ERNEST BASIL,

A NOVEL.

BY

J. McGRIGOR ALLAN,

AUTHOR OF " THE WOMAN-HATER ; OR, TRUE AND
FALSE LOVE," &c.

*" Avez-vous été dans votre vie six mois malheureux par
amour dirais-je à quelqu'un qui voudrait lire ce livre."*
DE STENDHALL, *(Henri Beyle). Phys. de l'amour.*

IN THREE VOLUMES.

VOL. I.

LONDON :

T. CAUTLEY NEWBY, PUBLISHER,

30, WELBECK STREET, CAVENDISH SQUARE, AND
OLIVER AND BOYD, EDINBURGH.

1857.

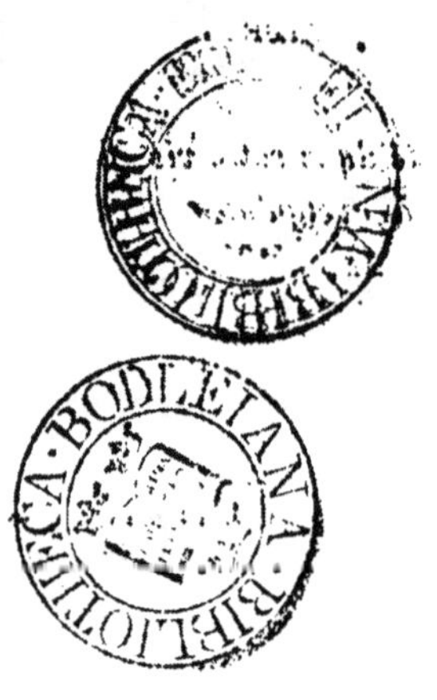

ERNEST BASIL.

PROLOGUE.

CHAPTER I.

THE STUDIO AND THE DRAWING SCHOOL.

ARTISTS are in general lofty birds literally in
their localities, they ought to be so in their
ideas also : let us hope that those who are *not*,
form the exception to the rule. Where they
most do congregate in New York, their studios
are generally at the top of the houses, so as to
enable them to get all the light possible. Up
you go, flight after flight of steps, till weary
and panting you arrive at a door with a couple
of bells—one belonging to a portrait painter,
Mr. Talbot, the other to a landscape painter,
Mr. Carlton. Both these artists take pupils

who work very amicably together in an apartment opening out of the lobby as you enter. In this room, in which several easels are standing, surrounded by casts, busts, studies in colour, and light, and shade, and all the paraphernalia of the art, two students are busy at work, the shorter of whom, named Paul Pearson, was a young man embodying the popular idea of an artist, short, pale, thin, but handsome, with dark elf locks, and piercing black eyes.

" What can be keeping Sir Joshua and the Prince ?" said he to his companion.

" Oh, they will be here presently. The Prince, you know, is always late. There's one of them now. I'll open the door, I'm the nearest."

" Well, brothers of the brush," said the new comer, styled Sir Joshua, a tall young man with striking and intelligent features ; " future Raphaels, Titians, and Michael Angelos, how do you get on? I'm rather late to-day. I must make haste and get to

work before Talbot comes in." And he proceeded to open his colour box, and set his
pallette, that is, arrange the colours in order
upon it. "How's this?" he exclaimed, going up to a dish in which he usually saved his
colours, and finding no water in it. A loud
laugh was all the comfort he received.

"So that's the way you save colours is it,
Basil?"

"Pretty fellows you are; you might have
put some water over them. Laugh away,
though, you can't vex me to-day. I was at a
party last night, and danced with such a lovely
girl."

"Ah, the old story now Basil's come, we shall
hear of nothing but the girls," said Pearson.

"Introduce a better topic, then," said Basil,
"if you don't like it. Hullo, there's the
Prince."

The young gentleman so named had some
title to be considered an original. He had
taken it into his head to be an artist; but there
were three striking obstacles to his success:

talent for the art, of which he possessed little
or nothing; perseverance, of which he possessed still less; and money, of which he had
a great deal too much for a profession which
requires the strong spur of poverty as a stimulus to success. Augustus Vere (such was
his real name) mingled a good deal of conceit
with plenty of generosity, this gave him among
his artist companions the name of the Prince.
He was continually taking holidays, and going
to the opera instead of the drawing school.
Yet no doubts ever disturbed his mind about
his eventual success, and although he had been
with Talbot a year and a half, he had not yet
began to handle the brush, being confined to
making drawings in chalk and charcoal, yet
he would talk coolly about not exhibiting pictures till he became a master, in a way which
convulsed the studio with merriment. He was
so very deaf that you could converse in the
usual tone without any possibility of his hearing, and Basil frequently amused his fellow
pupils by the way in which he would give the

Prince a rowing in the style of their master, Talbot; when in one of his savage humours.

Vere, or the Prince, now entered the room booted and spurred, with a riding whip in his hand. His appearance was the signal for a general burst of mirth.

"So your highness has not come to stay. Merely to come the Lorenzo the Magnificent, or Charles the Ninth over us. Will you pick up my brush most august sovereign if I let it fall? Will it please your royal highness to take off your hat, lay aside your whip, and stay awhile?"

"Why didn't you bring up your horse, Vere?" said another.

The Prince looked a little confused at these compliments.

"Who wants tickets for the opera to-night?" he exclaimed. "Here's one a-piece," and he laid them on the table. "Can't stop to-day, old fellows, but to-morrow I am going to begin and work deuced hard. I say, you needn't mention to Talbot that I was here unless he should ask particularly.   Perhaps he'll think I'm ill."

"Oh, don't distress yourself," said Sir Joshua, for the benefit of the grinning students, " he is so accustomed to your absence he never misses you.   There, put another scratch on your drawing, or stay, I'll do it for you. Now your daily work is done and you may go play.   A line a-day is your quantum.   You may adopt the celebrated motto in its most literal sense—" *nulla dies sine linea.*"   Now hie away, votary of pleasure, unworthy trifler with the muse of art.   No true child of genius —no real aspirant to the fame of Michael Angelo and Corregio.   Disgrace, clog, stain to the profession, avaunt !—get thee hence— vanish !"   And Vere, who only knew by the amusement of the students that Basil was making fun of him, vanished amid a perfect storm of laughter.

" I confess I should like to see the Prince when he has become a master.   I shall expect to see many changes, and particularly in art, before that time !" and the laughter was redoubled at this sally.

" But he really thinks himself improving," said Pearson.

" Ah, you have a microscopic eye," said Basil. " It is by such infinitesimal degrees, that his progress is like a mathematical point, a thing which exists but in the imagination."

" Well, I think Sir Joshua's chaffing does him good," cried the tall student, whom they named Poussin, being a disciple of the landscape painter, " really he's getting to be as frightened of you as Talbot himself; yet he has made some progress since I came here."

" Yes, but if he doesn't get on faster he'll die of old age before he has a picture in the exhibition, especially if he waits to be a master as he threatens. The conceit of a chap talking in that way. He told me when I first came here—' I don't think Talbot will let you begin colours for the first half year, for I've been here a year and a half and I havn't begun yet.' "

The uninitiated reader must not suppose that the day's work was over when the students left Mr. Talbot's studio about four or five o'clock. By no means. After an interval, during which dinner or tea had been dispatched according to the fashion of the parties, they met again at seven at the drawing school.

This is a large apartment lighted from the top. Around the walls are arranged all the *chefs d'œuvre* of ancient and modern sculpture in plaster casts. Here is the lord of the unerring bow—the Farnese Hercules—the statue that enchants the world, torsos, busts, models of hands, limbs, feet, &c. Thirty or forty students are bending over their drawing boards, each endeavouring to imitate as closely as possible either with pencil, chalk, or brush, some model which has caught his fancy and admiration.

The scene is very impressive to a thinking mind. Deeply suggestive of thought these relics of a past civilisation now inspiring the youth of the present. The contrast between those grand immovable forms, which would seem in their matchless symmetry as if called into being with the rapidity of a wish, the offspring of a lightning flash of thought, or changed from life into stone, so true, so natural, are the attitudes and detail, the play of the muscles, the contour of the limbs, &c., the contrast between them and the stooping, living figures, disciplining and educating their tastes to a due perception of beauty, devoting themselves in youth voluntarily to a life of toil and deprivation, and imbibing by slow repeated efforts capacity to appreciate, and facility to imitate such immortal works, naturally suggests the brevity of life and the eternity of art.

Where are the intellectual giants who created from the shapeless rock these glorious forms. They live in their mental offspring more truly than in their living descendants. Generation after generation shall depart, while the poor clay they have moulded, the cold marble over which they poured out their inspiration, their hopes, their lives, shall speak to us with an eloquence far transcending that of human beings.

Underneath the room devoted to the students is a large billiard room, with a bar attached. Here are two specimens of young America. Above are the votaries of the muses—below are young men making cannons, drinking gin-slings, sherry-cobblers, mint-juleps, brandy-smashes, cock-tails, and many more extraordinary compounds.

Among the artists are a great variety; some well-dressed and respectahle in appearance, others looking as if they took up their night's lodging in the gutter. Some eager and earnest in the pursuit of their art, others negligent and vacilating! some silently working, others chatting and laughing; some wandering about endeavouring to fix upon a subject, dazzled as they may well be among so many beautiful objects; for there are two ways of studying, practically with the pencil as an artist, and the other dreamily through the contemplation and imagination as a poet. The Prince is not

here. He came the first night, and staid just
long enough to scrawl an absurd fantastical
figure upon his board, underneath which some
one has written " don't repeat such efforts."
A good many drawing-boards are turned to
the wall. These, if inspected, would be found
to contain paintings made in the life school.
Round one of these, a group of students are
collected, laughing at some remarks made by
Ernest Basil, who appears to be playing the
critic, and the conversation, though carried on
in a jesting spirit, is illustrative of the mercy
which artists show one another. It should be
borne in mind, that studies in colour made by
artificial light, are liable to present a very different appearance during the day and night.
The artificial light alters and confuses the colours so much, that the artist who has laid
aside his work tolerably satisfied over night, is
not unfrequently shocked and disgusted when
he comtemplates it by day light. This of
course applies to beginners.

" So, let's hear who Basil is slashing so unmercifully," said a student as he joined the group already laughing heartily as Ernest proceeded in his remarks.

" The author of this life-study, whoever he may be gentlemen, certainly deserves the prize for colouring as much as Vere does for drawing. If you could but see it in day light, it is worth coming here on purpose. I saw it this morning. The flesh is of an exquisite purple running into excruciatingly cold blue shadows, and the hair is of a beautiful olive green."

" Perhaps he intended to paint a flayed man and represent the arterial and veinous blood," said one.

" Oh, yes, give him time," added another, " he'll put on the skin next evening."

" According to that system he should have laid in the bones first, and then proceeded to the ligaments and the first layer of muscles."

" No doubt he was thinking of Titian's bunch of grapes when he painted the flesh."

" And of a mermaid when he painted the hair."

" Or else he grew disgusted with nature as Fuseli did, finding she put him out, and fell back on imagination.

" He certainly should receive a vote of thanks as well as the Prince, and be requested to take the office of professor of painting, and lecture on the art of colouring by artificial light."

Here one more good natured than the rest put in ;—" I heard him say he had never painted from the life before."

" That is very evident, and indeed I can believe it." And similar asperities followed in quick succession, interspersed with much laughter ; but Ernest continued.—

" A glorious triumph then for a first attempt. You see he leaves it out to challenge admiration, instead of turning it round to the wall like the rest. He intends it for a model. Look at and study it, gentlemen ; and he has never been back to the school since he did it. He is afraid to put another touch to it for fear of injuring the effect, the rich tone of colour.

"Basil, you are too bad," cried all laughing heartily nevertheless.

"He leaves this great work to represent him, and does it not indeed do so during his absence. Are we not admiring and criticizing it now more than all the others. Let him rest satisfied, his memory will not be forgotten, he need return no more as long as this remains. Shall we not cherish, gentlemen, this model of art so generously bequeathed to you, so highly original in its mode of treatment. I really cannot say to what school it properly belongs. The masses of warm and cold colour are laid in with a generosity which would have charmed Sir Joshua. Whether the artist intended to retouch it and give more effect to these exquisite purples and beautiful blues, or whether he leaves it as a representation of what flesh ought to be, is more than I can say; but let us be grateful to him for leaving it to our guidance and instruction, gentlemen"—Here the light diminishing, gave the signal for ceasing work, and laying aside drawing boards, &c. "The lecture is over, you are dismissed. We shall resume the same subject to-morrow." And amid the buzz of conversation and light-hearted merriment, the students seperated for the evening, and Ernest Basil went home to read himself asleep over Vusaris Lives of the Painters, or Benvenuto Cellini, or to dream of Michael Angelo, and Fra Angelico.

The time was now arrived when he was to leave Mr. Talbot's studio, and set up his easel independently as a portrait painter. The conclusion of his last quarter was celebrated by a little festive re-union consisting of his fellow pupils and a few other students. These little periodical gaieties were common at the close of each student's quarter, and were held in the studio, on which occasion, the pictures, casts, busts, &c., were disposed to the best advantage, and added, as it were, inspiration and effect to the scene. There is a delightful *abandon* in these feasts of reason and flows of soul, a charm which those who have mingled in them will not easily forget. On this occasion half a dozen good fellows, all young, ardent, and inspired with love for their art, had met together to celebrate the departure of one of their number, whose gaiety and good qualities, added to his merit as an artist, made him a general favorite. The hours sped away rapidly and everything went well, save that owing to the introduction of champagne in too great quantity by the Prince, a very young landscape student had at a very early part of the entertainment been put *hors de combat* and had been removed and put to bed in an adjoining room under the care of the old woman who " did out " the studio, anti-room, &c.

The Prince had risen with a very pompous air, and proposed the health of his very good friend Mr. Ernest Basil, popularly known among brothers of the brush as Sir Joshua, whom, he was proud to say, he had known long (about six months). The prince spoke for ten minutes eulogizing Mr. Basil in a strain of high-flown panegyric, which caused that gentleman to blush and laugh alternately. He concluded with saying that, " the honour of the profession would find a glorious supporter in one who, for unflinchingness of perseverance and study, for noble magnanimity, in conceiving an idea, and for thorough knowledge of manipulation to carry it out, might challenge the world to produce an equal; and he would say this of Mr. Basil, that he doubted not he would make a capital portrait painter after he had been to Italy and studied Van Dyck, and in the mean time he was a very first-rate fellow, and no mistake; indeed a regular brick." Here the Prince having exhausted his Demosthenic ability, sat down amid a storm of cheering and gingling of glasses, such as never before had been heard in the studio, and made the very pictures shake on the walls, and the busts to nod a sort of approval of the toast. After his health had been drunk with all the honours, Mr. Basil rose to reply.

" Gentlemen," he said " or rather fellow students, brothers in art if not in arms. If I were to say this was the happiest and proudest moment of my life, I should not only be guilty of very hackneyed plagiarism, but I should tell a pretty big falsehood into the bargain. I will not say that I may not have been happier and prouder than at this moment, though perhaps, I have seldom been more so, but there is one consideration which interferes with feelings of unalloyed gratification, and that is the thought that this is the last time I shall share the harmless mingling of sentiment and conviviality within these walls. Gentlemen, as the song says—

We've had some happy hours together.

We can I think all look back upon the past six months and say it has not been the idlest or the saddest portion of our lives. I devoutly wish that our future career and experience of art may have the same happiness in store for us. We have sat here day after day wielding our brushes while song and conversation made the hours pass cheerily away. Often and often have I compared this happy existence with the monotonous life of a counting-house clerk. Yet let

us enter into no invidious comparisons. In
my opinion the poor artist need not envy the
rich merchant, and I feel very certain that I
state a fact when I say that a rich merchant does
not envy a poor artist. Such, gentlemen is life.
' Things must be as they may be.' But with
regard to ourselves we have as yet every reason
to feel grateful and indebted to our profession.
Art has made us known to one another:
Art has kept us friends. And let us hope that
a friendship founded and cemented on a mutual
love of art will not be easily or lightly broken.
The time at last has come for one of us to go
out into the world and test the skill which he
has acquired. - That time will soon come for all.
Our companionship will be broken up; the
studio will see an entirely new set of faces.
But if in the fluctuations of that variable untried
sea of futurity which lies so temptingly before
us, any two of us should be cast together again,
I need not say, I hope, I feel sure that they
or we will meet as friends; that the thoughts
of the days when we imbibed knowledge and

truth and visions of beauty, side and by side,
and laughed and quizzed and bantered each
other, will never be forgotten.　You have many
of you been a witness of the battles fought between my friend Poussin there and myself in
defence of our respective countries, for which I
am sure we deserve respectively the gratitude
of Her Majesty Queen Victoria and the President of the United States.　But in the midst
of our little bickerings, which may indeed have
caused us to respect one another the more, there
has been one feeling, one tie of brotherhood at
bottom.　Need I say what that is?　Are we
not students aspiring to be, if not yet, *artists?*
It was then our love of art.　There we may
be said to have one common country—Italy.
Happy is it for artists to possess that common
ground on which they may for a time at least
lay aside all other nationality and feel all distinctions swallowed up in admiration of Michael
Angelo and Raphael, as they wander through
the Vatican, or lie gazing upon the ceiling of
the Sistine.　Gentlemen, I have one toast to

propose, in which I feel my friend yonder and all of you will heartily join—' May we meet in Rome.' "

The toast was drunk standing, and not without emotion, for Basil's speech, besides being pathetic, had touched the true chord of sympathy in their artist hearts. The tall American stretched his hand over and shook Ernest's in a friendly grasp. " May we meet in Rome," he says, and buries his face in his tumbler, and when he removes it his eyes glisten whether with the strength of the punch, or from some other cause, we know not. Then Ernest proposes the Prince's health, and the Prince gets up and returns thanks, and orders in more champagne, and apologises that he doesn't happen to have tickets for the opera for to-morrow evening. The tall American's health is proposed, who gets up, returns thanks, and glides into a national speech, in which he says he has lived in the British provinces, and he doesn't wish to live among nicer people than the colonists, and next to being a free and enlightened American citizen, he would be a British subject, and he will always speak well of England, as he doubts not his friend, Mr. Basil always will of America when he hears it unjustly assailed, and concludes by proposing as a toast—"England and America united against despotism and oppression." Then they sang — "Should auld Acquaintance," shaking hands all round, and Paul Pearson sings "Ben Bolt," and the Prince, who values himself upon a blighted attachment, and has been telling Mr. Basil privately that unless he marries the young lady who has jilted him, he never will marry at all, sings a very doleful and sentimental song, the burthen of which is, that people in general have been sent into the world for no other purpose but to suffer from blighted affections, which is succeeded by a roaring chorus of " We won't go home till morning," shortly after which the party breaks up and separates, after a severe ordeal of hand-shaking, and Basil walks home with the Prince, who never leaves off talking in a very unconnected strain all the way, speaking very thick, and occasionally sliding a whole sentence into one long comprehensive word, like the Greek, evidently under the impression that he is convincing Ernest of his sobriety—one moment assuring his companion that he will never marry anybody but Miss ——, at another sitting down upon the doorstep and spanning his ancle, saying with a triumphant look at Ernest as he makes his finger and thumb meet, " That is a sign of good blood !" whereat Ernest laughs heartily, and replies, " It is a sign of a small ancle," and having seen the Prince safe within doors, walks home dreaming of Raphael and future success, in the brilliant radiance of moon-light in New York.

CHAPTER II.

ERNEST BASIL IS BURNT OUT AND BEGINS THE
WORLD—NEW YORK.

ERNEST BASIL (whom we introduced so abruptly
to the reader's notice in our first chapter) was
the son of a British Officer.   Born in England,
he had left that country at too early an age to
have any recollections of it, and had received
his education entirely in the British Provinces.
He had left home at an early age, after having
completed a course of classical education at his
provincial university, and had spent some
years abroad travelling in the States and residing in Canada.   Shortly before our story
opens he had returned home and found himself,
between the age of twenty and twenty-one, in

what he almost looked on as his native town, without a profession. The colonies had lately undergone great changes. The people tired of seeing all offices of trust and consequence occupied by parties nominated from home (that is England) had taken these offices into their own gift and conferred them upon the principal and most deserving among the colonists. While thus very properly throwing open a field of ambition hitherto closed to the rising generation, the salaries were so reduced and the continuance of office made so dependant on the will of the people, that many young men (Ernest among the number) looked to a much wider sphere of labour for advancement in the world than the colony seemed able to bestow. About this time his friends discovered that he possessed a singular facility in drawing like-nesses and so many hints did he receive on all hands of the propriety of cultivating his talent, that he began at last to consider seriously whether he had not best devote himself to the art of portrait painting in earnest instead of

sketching likenesses of his friends for amusement as he had hitherto been doing.

The advice he received on this point was as
contradictory as that commodity generally is.
One party advised him to persevere through
thick and thin, others told him to distrust himself; some blew hot and cold with the same breath
and threw cold water on the hopes they had
just been raising; another who had been mainly
instrumental in encouraging and even in foster
ing his taste for art, was heard to regret that such
a fine young man should trust his hopes in life
to a profession in which he never could excell,
a speech which of course soon came to Ernest's
ears through the agency of some good-
natured friend: some already thought him an
Apelles on whom all instruction would be
thrown away, and others thought it a pity that
one who could hit off such striking likenesses
and such pretty sketches should not have the
advantages of a regular course of study.

In the mean time Ernest had resolved to be
a painter, had sent to Boston for oil colours

and sat himself down to educate himself as far as he could do so in a small town of five or six thousand inhabitants. Wistfully he thought of New York as presenting the best means of studying art on that side of the Atlantic and as far exceeding in all opportunities the out-of-the-way town in which circumstances for the time being compelled him to dwell, as *it* was in its turn excelled by European cities. By one of these freaks of fortune which seem to form eras in many men's lives an accident untoward and lamentable as it at first seemed, was destined to bring about his wish of going to New York. One of those fearful fires which so frequently devastate wooden towns in America was to be the means of effecting this exchange, by destroying the house in which he lived, along with two or three hundred others.

Ernest Basil was sitting in the room which he had appropriated under the name of studio to his as yet unfledged efforts in art, painting the picture of a young lady when the cry of fire reached his ears. In towns of this size it is necessary for every one to be on the alert against the terrible enemy of—*Fire*. He who would refuse his personal assistance to his neighbour on such an alarm, would not only be acting selfishly but foolishly, since to-morrow he might stand in need of the same assistance himself. But indeed there is an excitement in an affair of this sort which has an engrossing charm for the young and adventurous. Ernest made it a point to work zealously at all fires. At the first alarm he threw aside the brush and hastened to the scene of destruction, where already men of all conditions and ranks were assembled, both official, military, and religious, exerting themselves in carrying water, manning the engines and saving property. To one who has no interest at stake, a fire in a wooden town has a strikingly picturesque appearance. Long lines of citizens stretch down towards the river, or to wells, wherever water can be procured, in double rows, one of which passes the full buckets from hand to hand to the engines, while the other returns the empty to be refilled. In this apparently inefficient way and also by waggons, which are constantly going to and fro with water casks, many a fire is subdued when taken in time, which to an inexperienced eye, threatened to carry all before it. The military are called out and invariably do good service, some work at the engines, others mount guard over furniture and property lying about in the street, others are employed with axes hewing down houses to form a gap in the communication of the flames.

It was not till night had closed in, and his mother and sister were safely housed with kind friends, that Ernest found time to take food and repose, or to give a glance at his fortunes for the future. Next day it was settled that Mrs. and Miss Basil should depart without delay to take up their residence with a lady residing in Nova Scotia, a dear and valued friend, while Ernest should only remain behind long enough to settle their affairs, sell the remnant of furniture, pay off any outstanding debts,

arrange matters at the insurance office, and then
try his fortune as an artist in New York Thus
by a severe and unexpected loss of property his
wishes were fulfilled, so mingled is good and
evil in this world.   True he did not feel particularly happy at the way in which his departure had been brought about, but at one and
twenty man is a hopeful animal, and after the
painful parting with his mother and sister was
over, and he had heard tidings of their safe
arrival and domestication with their old friend,
he began to brighten up. The coming winter
would be spent profitably in New York, instead
of comparatively wasted as far as art was concerned. I shall not describe the severe and
sorrowful partings which Ernest had to go
through at quitting a place where he had
grown up from youth to manhood, and where
he was personally known to man, woman,
and child. There was yet another parting of
a more solemn nature. The last visit he

paid before embarking in the steamer was to the churchyard to look once more, perhaps for the last time, upon the grave of a father and a brother. Who could adequately paint the ideas that thronged tumultuously in his mind during the twenty minutes he spent here. Some one had been there before him that day and scattered flowers upon the grave of his brother. He well knew whose hand it was. The wind sighed mournfully through the branches of a tree which sheltered them as he took his last look and walked slowly away.

" Wear this ring, dear Ernest, in memory of our true and warm friendship," said his best and most intimate friend as the steamboat was on the point of starting which was to bear our young adventurer from the place so endeared by every tie that can hallow and bind, into the great world. The two friends wrung each other's hands. There were few words spoken, but each knew and felt the worth of what he was losing. The boat swung off—his friend's form grew indistinct among the crowd on shore—the windings of the river soon shut the well-known town from his view—and Ernest Basil was fairly launched upon the world.

CHAPTER III.

A NEW YORK BELLE—SOMETHING MORE THAN A
PLEASANT ACQUAINTANCE—TOUCH AND GO.

WE have now accounted for Ernest being a
student of art in New York, and brought our
story to the period represented in our first
chapter.

No wonder then if he enjoyed the change
from a town, comparatively speaking a village,
to New York. Here he went into society,
judged entirely by his own merits, without any
of those miserable restrictions to happiness
which mark a little community. After his relaxation from close study with Mr. Talbot, and
at the drawing school in the evening allowed
him opportunity to go more into company, he

made a greater progress in self-confidence and *savoir faire* in one winter than he would have done in ten years' residence in the colony.

Artists of the first ability are of course eagerly sought after in society everywhere, but in America and in New York the profession generally appears to stand higher than in England, and artists in general go more into what is called the " upper ten thousand," or by the *sans culottes* less elegantly, but expressively, " the cod-fish aristocracy."

The opening of the National Academy Exhibition of Paintings in New York is gene rally celebrated with a supper, to which all the exhibitors are invited, and where a great majority of the celebrities may be seen. On the occasion of Ernest exhibiting his first picture, a breach was made in the usual custom, and a *soirée* substituted instead of a supper. It was done to give greater *èclat* and popularity to the exhibition. Nevertheless, the artists grumbled a good deal. The ladies they said would always come, but such a supper with its accompaniment of toasts and speeches from some of the most eminent men in the union, was too good to be lost. Ernest, however, was too young and gallant to think so as he wandered through the rooms and observed the fair specimens of American beauty which met the eye in every direction, making even the exquisite female portraits of Elliott and Ingham look tame and insipid, for though the loveliness of American women does not last, there is a rare delicacy, a *spirituelle* about it, which may safely challenge competition with any country. He and the Prince wandered through the rooms together, for the latter, though not an exhibitor, had sufficient influence to be admitted. Ernest was dressed plainly and simply in a correct evening costume. The Prince, whose means allowed him to be very *recherché* in his dress, was in the extreme of young American fashion. His hat, which he carried into the room with him, had a brim wide enough almost for a quaker, his pants seemed to have been made on him, so excruciatingly close did they fit to his legs, his shoes were so blunt at the point that they appeared too short for his feet, the sleeves of his coat were very wide, and he wore lemon-coloured gloves which it had taken him an hour to get on. They met Pearson, who had a very nice little picture in the exhibition, and were sauntering round the room, criticising alternately the pictures and the living beauties, when Ernest felt his arm squeezed like a vice, while the Prince at the same time exclaimed, in a very tragical whisper,—

" There she is standing by her portrait. Hide me—let me escape from her observation."

Nevertheless, it became apparent very soon both to Ernest and Pearson that the Prince, so far from wishing to escape from the attention of the young lady, was extremely anxious to attract her notice. Ernest and Pearson both looked in the direction indicated by the Prince, and beheld a strikingly beautiful young lady standing at no great distance from her own portrait, as if she had no great objection to

convince the bystanders how far nature can
supersede art. At the same moment he heard
a lady say to her companion, a gentleman,
directing his attention to the picture—

" There is Miss Norton's picture, by ——.
Is it not beautiful ?"

" Beautiful indeed," said the gentleman,
with such a sudden and unusual energy of
manner, that the lady said—

" So I have at last excited a little artistic
furor. But what are you about? You are
not looking at the picture at all, you are looking at the original," she exclaimed in a peevish
tone of voice. " Conceited thing, standing
near her picture to be observed."

Ernest had heard all this, but he saw that
the Prince wanted to be questioned, so he said
innocently,—

" Who is the young lady ?"

" Don't you know ?—can't you guess ?—
that is the lady who—who—the one I have
told you of so often, who holds my destiny in
her hands, Miss Norton."

" Indeeed, she seems gracious enough now, at all events, she is smiling and nodding towards you." Ernest saw that Vere had gained his point in attracting Miss Norton's attention, and that he only wanted a little pressing to do what he most heartily wished to do, go up and speak to her. " You must go and speak to her, she evidently expects it."

" Do you think so, my dear fellow? Well, you and Pearson must come too, I never should have the courage to face her alone."

If the truth must be told, Miss Norton's encouragement and discouragement of Mr. Vere's affections were entirely the coinage of that young gentleman's imagination. He had for a long time fancied himself in love with Miss Norton—had looked upon the reception of sundry bouquets as a token that his passion, (which he thought he displayed in every look, gesture, and word,) was reciprocated, and had chosen to construe some real or fancied coldness on the young lady's part as a rejection of his suit, and immediately reported himself in confidence to all his friends, a martyr to blighted affection. As for Miss Norton, she was entirely ignorant of the havoc she had made with Mr. Vere's heart, whom she regarded solely in the light of an acquaintance who was very amusing in spite of his conceit. On the present occasion she entered into an animated conversation with Ernest as soon as he had been introduced to her. Miss Norton was so beautiful as to be considered one of the belles of New York, and many an artist had formed the foundation of future fame by sending her portrait to the exhibition. Often and often as she had been painted she was never tired of sitting, and considered every solicitation as a fresh triumph, for which her own sex did not spare her. Ernest had seen her picture before and wondered whether the original could be as beautiful as the painter had represented her. Now as he looked at Miss Norton he thought it almost a libel on her beauty. No wonder as he saw that eye sparkle—those lips disclose such pearly teeth—and that smile, those dimples in the cheek—and then the music of her voice—oh! these were beauties beyond the reach of art. He took care to express this to her, veiled of course in the usual indirect language of compliment, and what pretty woman was ever displeased with a compliment which her conscience or her vanity told her she deserved.

"I almost concur in condemning the presence of the ladies in the exhibition to-night, Miss Norton."

" Oh! Mr. Basil, can you be so ungallant? Why so, pray?"

" Not on the same grounds which I have heard urged by some of my brother artists, viz., that we can get the ladies to come at any time, but because when they come in such force they kill the pictures. As for me, with the blaze of living beauty before my eyes, I feel as if I should never care to look at a picture again. I used to fall in love with all Elliott's and Ingham's female portraits, but to-night, somehow, they have lost their charm."

" Do you like Elliott's portraits, with all that decided red and blue about them ? You know what *les méchants* say, that all Elliott's ladies drink and shave."

" I admit he does force the colour a little too much, but he does it with such exquisite skill, that for my part I wouldn't wish one of his ladies less red or less blue. I always think of Turner's answer to the critic, who said, timidly looking at one of his gorgeous effects of colour—' Really, Mr. Turner, it is very fine, but I never saw anything in nature like it.' ' No; but don't you wish you could ?' "

" Then Ingham's portraits are all painted in a broad light, and are so finicky, and have so little force."

" But what careful finish. He reminds me of Carlo Dolci."

After discussing the pictures, the conversation verged on other topics.

" Who are those remarkably dressed ladies there," said Ernest, directing the attention of

Miss Norton to a party of what are technically called Bloomers.

"That is the celebrated Mrs. B——, and her three daughters. Is it not a pity they should make themselves so conspicuous. It is all their mother's fault. She is so old she may do as she likes, but she should have some regard for her daughters' feelings."

"It certainly looks better on the young than the old. I hope you will not think me particularly *outré*, if I confess I have a partiality for the Bloomer costume. If it was not for the prejudice which attends all innovation, I think the ladies would like it. Unfortunately, it has got mixed up in their heads with the idea of female emancipation."

"Take care," said Miss Norton, laughing, "perhaps I may be one of the new school."

"So that is the celebrated Mrs. B——," said Ernest, "How gloriously independent she looks as she moves among the throng, as much as to say, think what you choose. She certainly deserves credit for her courage at any rate. Some of the ladies are looking at her as if they would like to commit an assault."

" That is just her character, Mr. Basil. She does not care ten cents what you or I, or all the world thinks of her. She has put herself at the head of a moral revolution. I don't believe she, or her party, if asked point blank, could tell you distinctly what they want women to do, or what her mission is. Nevertheless, they never stop agitating, discussing, calling meetings, and writing books on woman's needs, woman's rights, woman's wrongs, and woman's mission, and such stuff as that. I only know," continued Miss Norton, " I am very happy, and don't want any more liberty or right than I have."

" It is not every one that possesses Miss Norton's personal and mental endowments, and have therefore the same inducement for content," said Ernest, bowing.

" Pray, Mr. Basil," said Miss Norton, abruptly changing the subject, " how long is it

since you have left England. I like the English.
I once knew such a nice British officer and his
lady, and they gave me such accounts of
England, that I quite longed to go there."

" I am glad to hear you say you like my
country, Miss Norton, but you must not suppose I am directly from England. An Englishman by birth, I am a colonist by education.
A colonist, you know, is a strange creature,
neither fish nor flesh. He adores England,
yet Englishmen hardly recognise his existence,
and he is little better known in the United
States. I'll wager you never heard the name
of my province. Did you ever hear of New
Brunswick."

" Why, I have been in New Brunswick in
New Jersey State."

" But that is not my New Brunswick, which
is a province, with a governor, and a parlia-
ment, and a regiment quartered in it, and I
don't know what all besides. For colonists
are very grand people I assure you within their
own colony."

" And do you like the colonies or the States best."

" Who could help liking New York,"

" You should go to some of our fashionable watering places, Saratoga, or Newport, during the season, if you want to see American society."

The conversation now happening to grow rather national, Ernest hazarded a remark which elicited from Miss Norton a display of that love of country which is such a characteristic feature in all Americans without distinction of class, age, or sex.

" What a pity America, by abolishing all distinctive marks of merit in the shape of titles or hereditary honours, should with-hold a strong inducement towards advancement which European countries possess."

" Titles, or orders of nobility," said Miss Norton, with a flashing eye, " it is our boast that we do not require—that we have outsoared those vestiges of an inferior civilization—that we have no privileged classes to eat up and oppress the people—that every citizen in this great country has a fair chance in competing for the highest offices. Our President was a poor boy working at a trade. Is not that a proud boast for any country."

" But you stand alone in studiously affecting to scorn all titles or order of merit."

" No matter, we do not follow other nations, we lead. Is not our country already the home of the destitute and the oppressed, the glory, the pride of the earth."

O love of country, thou hast thy weak side, but who can find fault with the sentiment which is the foundation of so much virtue. Ernest respected the prejudices of his beautiful antagonist. Like her, he had been taught to think *his country* the first in the world. To define patriotism would be difficult, nevertheless the man who has travelled and lived abroad, can form a better idea of it, than he who has not. Ernest had never loved his country more than now, when he lived under the Stars and Stripes, and heard England daily spoken of without those titles of friendship which her name had ever been coupled with before.

The Prince was not jealous of Ernest's long chat with Miss Norton. His deafness precluded him from taking much share in the conversation; but he had a good excuse for being near, and watching the motion of Miss Norton's lips, by which he could often give a shrewd guess at what she said, and imbibing fresh intoxication from the witchery of her presence. As for Pearson he would have forgot the greatest beauty in the world beside a picture.

Miss Norton's father lived in one of the finest houses in Fifth Avenue, which is the Piccadilly and Park Lane and Belgravia of New York. He was a merchant who had made an immense fortune by a lucky speculation and who now took his place among the upper ten thousand and gave entertainments and lived in a style which many a peer might have deemed extravagant. One brilliant moonlight night as Ernest was returning home he stopped to listen to one of those serenades so common in the streets of New York and which consist not of a love-sick individual accompanying himself to his guitar but of exquisite music discussed by a band of skilful performers stationed by some gallant admirer under the window of his lady love. Ernest was not a little surprised to recognize in the giver of this moonlight serenade the Prince. " Oh Basil is this you, I am so glad to see you. Do you see up at that window there, it's she I'm sure and that's her cousin Miss Larkins from the country. They'll ask us in directly. It's the custom, and give us a deuced good champagne supper into the bargain. Somehow or other I should have felt scared at going in alone. Old Norton would have been too many for me. But now I've you to back me I shan't mind."

" Me !" said Ernest considerably astonished, " they won't ask me, but how could I possibly go if they did. I don't know Mr. Norton and it's not likely one of the ' upper ten' will trouble himself about a poor artist."

" That's all you know about it said the

Prince. Old Norton is a devilish good fellow and knows how to spend money as well as make it and you mustn't measure us here by your aristocratic English notions."

And while they were speaking, as the Prince predicted, an invitation came from Mr. Norton with his compliments and he would be happy if Mr. Vere and his friend would walk in. In they went accordingly and in a very spacious apartment furnished and decorated in the French style, sat Miss Norton, her father and Miss Larkins. Miss Norton seemed very glad to see Ernest and introduced him to her father and her friend Miss Larkins. Mr. Norton was one of these men who, without the advantages of education have risen from nothing, to use a common phrase, through shrewd mother wit and who carry their prosperity well, giving themselves no airs, and therefore eschewing vulgarity, which consists in pretensions. His homely but frank manners formed a strange but pleasing contrast to the splendour which surrounded him. If Miss Norton had looked

beautiful at the *soiree*, she looked bewitching
to-night habited in such a becoming demi-
toilette; her exquisitely fitting dress, not permitting a particle of the neck or shoulders to
be visible, but displaying the beautiful figure to
perfection, and also the whole of the arm,
which in whiteness and contour formed a study
for a painter or a sculptor.   The hair was taken
off the face, in that style so peculiarly trying
to plain features, but so becoming to beauty.
In a very short time supper was announced by
a black footman in as near an approach to livery
as Republican prejudices would sanction, and
they adjourned to another elegant apartment,
where a hot supper awaited them, and no lack
of champagne; meanwhile the band played an
air from La Somnambula.   The whole thing
had been so sudden, the exchange from the
quiet lonely saunter in the moonlight to this
brilliantly lighted saloon, with all the accom-
paniments of beauty, wine, and music, that
Ernest felt not a little like Abon Hassan
when he woke up from his dream and found

himself in the Caliph's palace. As he walked home that night along with the Prince, thinking New York an enchanted city, he built some very lofty castles in the air.

Two days after he left his card at Mr. Norton's, and had the felicity of hearing Cæsar say that the young ladies were in. Miss Norton was reading a newspaper intently when Mr. Ernest Basil was announced. She laid it down hastily and her cheek flushed as she held out her hand.

" Pray, Mr. Basil," said Miss Norton, after they had conversed some minutes upon common-place topics, " are you at all literary? I often fancy from some of your remarks that you can be very critical and severe. I hope you are taking notes in private of us demi-civilised transatlantic folks to hold up to the derision of your countrymen."

Ernest hardly knew whether she was complimenting or quizzing him. He bowed as he replied somewhat coldly—

" That from the little he had yet seen of

America, he should be sorry to put any forward opinions, even if he felt otherwise qualified to to do so."   But, he added, " that his literary tastes had been obliged to give way to the pressure of art."

" Ah, you do write then," said Miss Norton. " I do wish some good-natured Englishman would write a book about us and remove some of the prejudices against us, which is not to be wondered at when we consider the atrocious libels on our habits and manners which have been hitherto published."

" I agree with you there, Miss Norton; but every day makes England and America better acquainted."

" I should like to know what you have been writing about us in New York in your journal; what your first impressions of the Yankees were. It is pleasant to know what intelligent foreigners think of us."

" How strange it seems to hear oneself called a foreigner in a country where they speak your language, and make one feel so soon at home."

" Now if you would only keep all your flattery for your book, about America, I am sure that it would sell well."

" Flattery would be appreciated from a recognised author, but from ' a youth to fortune and to fame unknown,' it would be wasted."

" But you are not a youth to fortune and to fame unknown, Mr. Basil ; but perhaps you have not seen to-day's paper."

" No, I have not."

" I am glad of it, for I shall be the first to announce good tidings. Look there," said Miss Norton, taking up the paper and handing it to him.

Ernest read as follows :—" We sometimes visit the gallery of the old masters belonging to the National Academy, and occasionally perceive a young artist disciplining his pencil and his taste in imitating their beauties. Mr

Ernest Basil has completed a very admirable copy of Raphael's Fornarina."

" Papa saw it first, and drew my attention to it. I am very glad you had not seen it until you came here. You see you are growing famous. We shall hear of you one day becoming a Royal Academician, for I suppose you will desert America altogether for Europe, where art is so much further advanced?"

" Well, I have my dreams of ambition, but unfortunately I know so many instances of artists struggling on with wives and families in indigent circumstances, that I often build castles of another character, perhaps quite as visionary, viz., marrying a rich heiress and so becoming independent of my art."

Miss Norton tried to rally Ernest upon being such a recreant votary of art, but she blushed a little nevertheless.

Ernest's sojourn in New York now began to grow exceedingly pleasant, and to give symptoms of being also profitable. Through the

Nortons he grew acquainted with several agreeable families, and sitters began to drop into the
studio, which he had lately opened. He likewise numbered a good many young lady acquaintances, which was perhaps the reason that
he did not surrender his heart altogether to
the charms and fascinations of Miss Norton,
which, under other circumstances, might have
been the case. About this time sundry little
triangular notes and other billets on scented
paper poured in upon him, and as this was a
kind of correspondence which had always possessed a greater charm for him than business
letter writing, he really began to grow very
much attached to New York, as his letters to
his sister and mother decidedly evinced. It is
certain that in his letters to his sister he often
took up half a page in describing Miss Norton's
personal appearance, and entered into great
detail on the subject of her dress, as he said to
convey to her an idea of a New York belle;
but Miss Basil, who was herself engaged, no
doubt, drew her own conclusions, and wrote to

Ernest that whoever he married, would be to her as a sister. Mrs. Basil, however, did not like the idea of her son losing those salutary prejudices against the Yankees which are cherished in good colonial society. It was not, therefore, without a secret pleasure that she received a letter from Scotland which required, or appeared to her to require, her immediate presence there. She determined that her son should accompany her after her daughter's marriage. His talents would soon enable him to make his way, particularly in the place where his parents had been known, and where she yet possessed so many friends and connections, and she knew that a visit to Scotland and England had long been a cherished wish of Ernest's heart.

Thus it came to pass that in following Ernest's career we are compelled to change the scene from the new to the old world.

Ernest had spent upwards of two years in New York happily and not unprofitably. It could not be expected that he could abandon

kind friends, sever so many pleasant friendships, and yield up so many hopes and prospects without considerable regret. Even the
thoughts of returning to his native country,
and the wonders awaiting him there, could not
stifle sorrow. Among the letters which he did
not burn, was one in a lady's handwriting,
which ran as follows :—

" DEAR FRIEND.—I write to you because
you are going away—because in a very short
time the pleasure of memory will be the only
frail link between us. Be assured I appreciate the motive which led you to decline the
invitation to our house last evening, and to absent yourself so much of late. Do not imagine Miss Larkins has betrayed any confidence
She merely told me enough of the conversation which passed between you to hinder me
from thinking that the alteration in your conduct proceeded from caprice—to let me see
that it proceeded from the best, the noblest,
the most disinterested motives. Yes, you are
right, it is best that we are are not to meet

again. My father is obstinate in wishing me to marry an American only. Yet I am glad I have known you, and that I am convinced there are men in the world who can act disinterestedly and nobly. Why should I hesitate to tell you, now that we are never to meet again, that it is better for my peace of mind that it should be so. The laws of society are very hard upon us women. We are expected to look upon all men with cold indifference, until one has singled us out to propose to, and then, if he be eligible, to change at once into the fond passionate adoring creature. From what I know of you, I shall not sink one iota in your esteem for writing this. You do not admire the mincing prudes, who, without taste and judgment to have a preference for one man over another, sit by in pretended indifference, while their mamas plot and scheme for them. After all, what is the difference between honestly writing or telling your preference, and constantly *acting* it by all those arts and shifts which society permits? A girl may dance night after night with a man,

and listen and talk nonsense to him by the
hour, but she dare not whisper unto herself,
' I love him,' lest Mrs. Candour should visit
her with his displeasure. It seems very strange,
but I dare say it is very right, that we require
so much more stringent laws than the gentlemen to keep us in order. You happy beings
may go abroad and forget your loves in new
flirtations, but we poor creatures must pine in
hall and bower. Pray burn all my scraps of
poetry. I send you one more—the last:

> " Farewell, but never from my heart
>   Shall time thine image blot ;
>   The dreams of other days depart,
>   Thou shalt not be forgot.
>
>   And never in the suppliant sigh
>   Poured forth to Him who rules the sky,
>   Shall my own name be breathed on high
>   And thine remembered not."

Ernest, like most *young* men, had carried
on many silly flirtations, when he believed that
the other party was no more serious than himself, and that it was done mutually *pour passer
le temps;* but there was something too noble
in his mind to permit him to become that de-

graded thing, whether man or woman, a flirt. As he grew older, and better acquainted with human nature, he could not help perceiving the fatal influence which one mind may have over another, and the consequent sin of thus sporting with the destiny of a human being. Some might have thought him vain and conceited for the conduct he had pursued towards Miss Norton, but his own conscience taught him he had done right. She was an heiress, the Prince loved her to desperation, and her father would disinherit her if she married a foreigner. Under these circumstances, the possibility of him, a poor artist, being the cause of unhappiness or disappointment to more than one, sufficiently indicated to him the course he ought to follow It was at this crisis his mother's letter arrived, and by unfolding the new prospects in view, served to confirm and second his resolution, which a longer residence in the same town with Miss Norton might possibly have caused to flag.

He was a good deal affected with the manner

in which the Prince received the news of his speedy departure.

"Going to leave New York, where you are so well known and getting on so well? Going to cut all your artist cronies?—no more oyster and champagne suppers—no more spouting?—or, can it be," he stopped, and then went on with the privilege of an old friend, " can it be, Ernest Basil, that you have proposed and been rejected by Eleanor Norton?"

"Nothing of the sort, my dear fellow "——

The Prince seemed labouring under great agitation, at length he spoke—

"I cannot make it out, Basil; if you had told me you were to be married to Miss Norton, I would have believed you. I have long lost hope in that quarter; though," he added, with a tone of emotion which invested his short stature with dignity, "I have not ceased to love her either, and—I could have wished you joy of it, my friend, I could. She's too good for me. I can make her laugh; but you—hanged if I don't think she loves you, and I've sometimes wondered you didn't speak out. Do you think I have no eyes in my head. When you first began to fight shy of coming to the house, I thought you might have had some explanation or other·"

"Prince," (for he had got into the way of calling him by his nickname) said Ernest, "Miss Norton is everything that is noble and good, but," he added, as he rung his friend's hand, "she is not too good for you. Forgive me," he added, "if I have ever unconsciously cost you a pang in that quarter. We are dear friends and nothing more."

It was evident by the sudden radiance which illumined the Prince's countenance that the honest fellow's heart was considerably lightened by this intelligence, and he began to chatter away in the satisfaction of his feelings, not observing the pre-occupied and rather melancholy look which his friend's features wore.

We will suppose all the adieus, and the regrets, and the promises of remembrance with which Ernest left New York, and bade adieu to friends, to convivial artist meetings, pleasant evenings spent at theatres and private parties. He did not know till the time for separation how much he had valued Pearson, who, though not so gay as the Prince, had a deep love for art, which united Ernest and himself in bonds of sympathy.

ERNEST BASIL.

PART I.

CHAPTER I.

Y——, we suppose was neither better nor
worse than other provincial towns either in
England or Scotland :—It had its editors who
spoke of it as our good city and sent forth
weekly strictures upon politics and morals for
the guidance, not merely of the provincial sphere
in which their papers circulated, but for the
benefit of the world at large, and occasionally
maintained their credit as oracles with their sub-
s cribers by a fearful onslaught upon some unconscious author or man *out* of office. It had
its acknowledged aristocrats moving like " mag-

nificent refrigerators" within their own orbits, and its would-be aristocrats toadying most diligently those above and frowning with infinitely greater superciliousness than those they aped, upon the class beneath : it had its fair proportion of bigots who thundered against every religious foible but their own ; its share of venemous spinsters who thrived on tea and scandal, and did good service to the cause of *morality*, or, at any rate, of *hypocrisy*, by the fear which their tongues inspired ; of milk-and-water and bread-and-butter young ladies who made the fear of the aforesaid spinsters or public " *censores morum*" serve instead of more profound principles, whose conversation and accomplishments breathed the happy atmosphere of mediocrity ; also of young gentlemen who did duty certain hours of the day in the principal street of Y——, sucking the nobs of their canes and acting as walking advertisments of their tailors by exhibiting the last year's London fashions in coats, pantaloons, and boots, &c. There were also the usual number of young gentlemen going through a regular course of tuition in the noble art of dissipation, living or rather dying on whiskey, abstracting door bells and knockers and *chaffing* policemen, and of young hypocrites who sinned less openly and passed themselves off on deluded mamas and maiden aunts as steady young men.

In this respect Y——— did not differ materially from other English or Scotch or Colonial towns but in no town that he had yet seen did religious bickerings run so high, as the following extract from one of his letters written to a confidential friend about this time will testify.

" In the first place there is the great implacable feud between Papist and Protestant and the Calvinist and Episcopalian, while each of these latter churches are split into two distinct branches, the one into the free church and established Kirk of Scotland, the other into Tractarian or Semi-Papal, and Evangelical or Semi-dissenting. As an Episcopalian I am almost at a loss what church to go to for the Episcopal body here are represented by three distinct congregations remarkably independent of each others tenets and forms of worship. First there is St. Annes Chapel of which Mr. Formula is encumbent. He is a rigid Tractarian carrying out the innovations upon usage to the utmost verge of the limits permitted by the rubric. He has equipped his handsome little chapel with all the gew-gaws and filagree and gingerbread work which his school of Christianity has of late begun to consider so essential to the true faith in reviving the spirit of the Primitive Church *who worshipped under the arch of heaven,* but which other Christians find so offensive that they go away disgusted to other churches. It is amusing to witness the effect of these gradually increasing decorations and changes in the method of conducting service on the variously prejudiced among the congregation, some of whom took fright at the first eruption of Pusyism, while others swallowed the intoning of the service, the lights upon the altar, with difficulty, and stand prepared to rebel and withdraw their allegiance on the ap-

pearance of the next novelty, while many have
the most unshaken confidence in their pastor,
and are determined to go to *Rome* with him if
absolutely necessary. The bishop's lady used
to attend this chapel, but the introduction of a
reading stand in the form of an eagle proved
too much for her over-wrought feelings. (It is
the last straw that breaks the camel's back.)
" That ever I should hae lived to see this day,"
she exclaimed, as she hastened out from among
them, considering it a merciful intervention of
providence that the roof has never fallen upon
such *Idolaters*. But Mr. Formula cares not
who goes or stays, and calmly equal to either
future, whether the outsides praise or blame
him, he has his faithful little flock who will
never be enticed away, and so long as he can
save them, it appears he is practically indifferent
to the fate of all the rest of mankind ; he is
continually devising how he can follow out the
rubric more strictly, and have fresh ornaments,
more striking and decided innovations, and
snaps his fingers (metaphorically of course) at

his Bishop, and dares him to interfere. He is a grim looking man, one of those who in the "*good old times*" would have sent a heretic, or a malignant to the stake as soon as he would have taken a glass of port wine ; a living witness in short of the danger of intrusting poor human bigots with power. There is something very orderly in the appearance of the congregation, all sitting on benches that face one way, and the service is performed with solemnity. Independently of his bigotry, Mr. Formula is a very good member of society, charitable to the poor, and brings up his family soberly and strictly. Nevertheless, he is always spoken of by his brethren of other denominations in Y——, as if he were a malefactor returned from Botany Bay before his time.

The bishop's church is the happy means between the ultra-tractarian and ultra-evangelical. It is a handsome building with no superfluous ornament. The pews are very commodious *for the rich*, being fitted up with curtains, cushions, and affording the occupants an opportuniiy of staring each other in the face instead of the clergyman. A Mahomedan or any other *barbarian* unacquainted with the mode of worship, might think they fully answered the purpose for which they were designed, viz. to sleep in. There are hard benches for the poor, The bishop never interferes with any of his clergy, having unfortunately excommunicated one who brought an action against him for consequent injury to his reputation, and obtained a verdict which cost the poor bishop fifteen hundred pounds. It is hard to define a bishop's power now a-days.

I now come to the congregation of St. James, where the excommunicated clergyman, the Rev. Mr. Stickler officiates. He happens to be at daggers drawing with the assistant clergyman, the Reverend Mr. Fluent, and as the congregation have entirely separated themselves from the jurisdiction of their bishop, there is no restraining power to awe those two belligerents, or to prevent the recurrence of scenes scandalising to a Christian community, and the remnant who still attend the church have no resource but to watch the continual wrangling between these two precious examples of Christian teachers, one of whom actually refused to receive the cup from the hands of the other at the communion table. As might be expected, the congregation is split into two factions, one in favour of Mr. Stickler, the other for Mr. Fluent, and each decides according to their respective prejudices, for one or the other. It is in vain to represent to them, that both parties have by their disgraceful disregard of the first principles enjoined by their religion, disqualified themselves from the title of followers much less of *teachers* of the gospel, or . to ask how the service conducted by two clergymen with hearts full of enmity can be anything but a mockery, how either can presume to pray or to minister to their fellow-men before their Creator, or exhort those to whom they offer a warning instead of an example.

Mrs. Basil and her son resided in furnished

lodgings at the house of Mrs. Saunders, the
widow of a merchant who had died bankrupt and
broken hearted, and left a wife and two daughters to experience the tender mercies generally
accorded by time-serving society under such
circumstances.   Miss Saunders was a very
superior and accomplished girl; the younger
sister had not received so good an education,
and was much more shy and reserved.

Ernest was not an early riser, as he often
read or wrote far into the watches of the night.
It was after nine o'clock, and Mr. Basil's little
handmaid had knocked more than once to ap-
prize him that his mother was not waiting
breakfast.

But even after Mr. Basil had descended, it
was no such easy task to get the breakfast over.
His appetite was never very keen, and temptation
awaited him in the shape of Miss Saunders who,
attired in a most becoming demi-toilette, was
occupied at this hour in whisking off imaginary
specks of dust from the furniture in the room
of their only other lodger.   A *téte-a-téte*

with this young lady before breakfast had from habit became the essential order of the day with Ernest, and it was enlivened by criticisms upon the passing belles of Y—— as the latter performed their matutinal shopping, for (Grafton St. was the principal thoroughfare of Y——), and prolonged in spite of the expostulations of Mrs. Basil, who frequently came in person to represent the heinous sin of permitting the breakfast things to remain on the table " at this hour of the day." Sometimes this objection was obviated by ordering the breakfast things into the lodger's room and despatching it there.

The real possessor of this apartment was as mythological, a being in the eyes of Ernest as the celebrated Mrs. Harris herself. Mr. Stuart was, so far as Ernest could learn, a human machine of that description generally typified under the title of a methodical man of regular habits—one of these bipeds born to put pens behind their ears, to be innocent of latch-keys, and whose soul, according to the transmigration doctrine, would find itself more at home in a clock-case than anywhere else—one of those slaves in short, not of the lamp, but of the chronometer, who render up their free will to that extremely useful instrument which marks the progress of time. He might have been personified by an hour-glass. He was never in his room after nine in the morning, never at home a minute earlier or later than four for dinner, migrated again immediately after this meal had been despatched, and returned to subside into his couch exactly at ten p.m. Such was the regular and harmless life led by Mr. Stuart. Ernest had never seen him, never expected to see him, never wished to see him. He was not a character to excite curiosity. Probably his existence was at times forgotten by Ernest except when a vague feeling of gratitude penetrated his soul towards the unknown individual who virtually accommodated him with the use of his apartment, while he the nominal proprietor paid the rent. For though Mr. Stuart, who it is needless to say was an old bachelor, had been an inmate of Mrs. Saunders' lodgings more years than Ernest had been months, he had not probably spent so many hours in his own apartment as the latter. Certain it is that those who saw Ernest lounging at the window, or sketching likenesses of the Misses Saunders or telling stories or heard the astounding bursts of merriment which occasionally proceeded from a bevy of fair visitors, could have come to the very correct and logical conclusion that Mr. Stuart the methodical man of business was not the presiding genius of the place. If some *fairy* had *peached* to the proprietor on his return, or if by any imaginable possibility Mr. Stuart had returned at an irregular hour, or if the echoes could have prolonged the words spoken, the jokes uttered and the laughter which exploded in the sacred apartment, who shall undertake to describe the amazement of the *prejinct* Mr. Stuart. Occasionally the trespassers would trench too closely on those witching hours at which the bachelor returned ; the creak of his square-toed shoes coming up the outer stair would give dreadful note of warning to Alice in the kitchen, and she would come flying in a breathless haste to utter the talismanic words " Mr. Stuart's coming up the stairs."   Instead of his foot having music in it, it caused confusion and dismay and great would be the scampering for a brief period until after the innocent cause of the rout had retired, when the room would resume its original jocund festivity and the echoes would again vibrate to hilarity and mirth.

One day Ernest as usual had come down humming an opera air and begun a lively dia- logue with Miss Saunders which had gradually merged in misanthrophy ; he had arrived at the conclusion that he was the most miserable being in the world without friends or sympathy and that he had a right to feel like another Timon of Athens, when Miss Saunders interrupted him. " Now if you will be so melancholy I shall not tell the good news I have for you."

" What is it ?"

" Why I have got a letter from Miss Lawrence and she is coming to-day.

" What your beautiful friend from Abercorn that you have been telling me of?   If she is as beautiful as you say I shall lose my heart."

" She is very beautiful," said Miss Saunders, " though rather shy with strangers, but you must not make love to her, for I'm not going to have her return to Abercorn broken-hearted for such a desperate flirt as you are."

Ernest had pictured to himself some how or other a very uninteresting country girl in Miss Lawrence.   He was therefore quite unprepared for the specimen of classical beauty which met his eyes when first introduced to the young lady whose arrival had been so anxiously expected.

Elinor Lawrence appeared to Ernest's artist gaze a perfect model of beauty.   Her features presented the pure classic outline of the Greek ideal ; but how far beyond the power of art to render was the changing colour of her dark Italian complexion—those glorious black eyes, whose flash was tempered by the long dark eye-lashes — and the raven tresses which would not be confined to any prescribed mode of fashion, but fell partly over her neck with a wild luxuriance which tended not a little to complete the resemblance of the whole head to an antique piece of sculpture.

How devoutly Ernest wished, as he noted all this in one sweeping comprehensive glance, that such a lovely being possessed a mind to correspond; but when he found all his efforts to draw out Miss Lawrence unavailing, he mentally and prematurely decided that she was but a beautiful statue, and nothing more. Long accustomed to a frankness of manner in young ladies, which in many instances permitted a superficial mind to be thoroughly estimated in the course of half an-hour's conversation, Ernest frequently jumped at conclusions which time proved erroneous.

" Will you two people never have done playing chess when you have sensible company to converse with ? I have drawn Miss Lawrence's profile three times while you have been at that one game."

"Do be quiet, Ernest, and leave us to finish our game," said Mrs. Basil.

So Ernest made another outline of the head of his beautiful sitter, who was occupying herself with a book, and by the time he had finished, the game was over. One never-failing topic of discussion between Ernest and Miss Saunders, was the existence of true love. Ernest had a serious way of taking the opposite side of any question, and it was difficult often to discover when he warmed with his subject whether he was speaking in jest or earnest.

"Trust me, Miss Saunders—take my word for it, and don't dignify by the name of love every evanescent attachment between empty-headed young men, and insipid young women. Just consider the way in which matches are made : a chance acquaintance, the interference of friends, the temptation of a little money, or a bit of land, or a few trifling flimsy accom-plishments, and you must confess that two people who marry and live together for the remainder of their lives only owe to chance that they do not live single and hate one another. A young gentleman and a young lady are engaged. Fortune smiles—they are both well to do in the world—everyone says they were made for one another—the day is fixed—the mama has given her consent. Suddenly the gentleman calls and announces that he has lost all and become a beggar. He is immediately turned to the right-about by the mother, the daughter goes into hysterics of three-young-lady power. After a week or so writes her lover a letter—very sorry—esteem—sacrifice—inclination to duty, and so forth, and the affair is at an end. Take another instance : two lovers have vowed by everything vowable to be constant for ever and ever. The man goes away, and after a certain number of years' absence, it is reported he is dead. He returns to find his disconsolate lady-love married to another."

" Well, and would not the gentleman do the same ?" interrupted Miss Saunders.

" To be sure he would, quite right—constancy is nowhere to be found in either sex. What has become of the unchangeable fidelity —of all those heaven-attested oaths, angel-witnessed promises which passed between them ? A few paltry years and they end in smoke. Well, they are guiltless, irreproachable ; they only attempted what they were unable to perform. Moral : it does not do for mortals to make such fine promises for the future ; Cordelia, the most constant of the sisters, doubted her power of loving more than all, and we may see instances every day of high-minded and refined people hesitating to bind themselves by a promise, which the majority of the race, inconstant and fickle, are ever ready to do. This is the way a philosopher would write on love and marriage, if you could fancy a philosopher writing of such things. He might say : love and marriage constitute a serious hallucination, which cause a man to make the most absurd promises, and put the most absurd faith in the promises of another.

E 2

He swears to be true till death, and finds it exceedingly difficult to remember the lady through six weeks of absence. Every man in love will gravely assert things which he knows to be mathematically false. That his affianced or his wife is the best and handsomest woman in the world, and that he is the happiest man. Every Mr. Tompkins or Mr. Smith says the same thing. Yet does not chance regulate our love affairs? Is not marriage a perfect lottery? If we reside in any town or city long enough, and are of a marrying turn, we must marry some woman living there or staying there temporarily. Yet next door to us may have lived one whom we should have loved ten thousand times better if we had known her. We may have seen the same woman a hundred and fifty times before we began to think her an angel, or even the best and handsomest woman in the world, or the only one we could possibly love. We may have been goaded on to the match by interested motives. We may be making diligent inquiries respecting the lady's *tocher*. We get

up in the morning an ordinary despairing
bachelor with our affections unengaged. In
the course of the forenoon we gain the required intelligence which decides us; we propose and are accepted, and at five o'clock precisely we have found the best and handsomest
woman in the world, and have become the
happiest man in the universe."

"How can you talk such nonsense, Ernest?"
said Mrs. Basil, "I am sure we would be better playing chess than listening to you."

"If your lot had been cast in the celestial
empire," continued Ernest, unmoved, "would
you not equally have found your phoenix there?
Ergo! Love affairs are regulated by chance,
and marriage is a lottery. As for me, I have
become so sceptical in these things, that the
very fact of people being engaged would in-
duce me to wager that they will never be
married."

Miss Lawrence listened attentively to all
this logic, and made no other reply than cast-
ing a glance of her lustrous orbs upon the

speaker, while Miss Saunders took up the cudgels warmly for her sex.

" Surely, Mr. Basil, you don't mean to say that you don't believe in a sincere attachment? If now a girl loved you faithfully, could you go away and forget her?"

Thus brought to a dead lock, Ernest would either evade the question with a joke, or, finding it impossible to escape without a serious reply, he would labour with all the eloquence in his power to remove the impression of his being a gallant gay Lothario, a bee roving from flower to flower, a knight who loves and rides away, or, to speak without metaphor, that most despicable of things a being without a heart.

" You do not exactly understand me yet, I see, Miss Saunders. In my effort to view a subject philosophically and rationally, I am obliged to include men and women in a broad comprehensive view, while I admit the existence of many exceptions. Though I have never been in love, I doubt not the existence of the passion any more than friendship, and just on the same principle that I would never forget those to whom I owe gratitude. I can conceive myself so bound to a female friend through years and years of absence. What annoys me is to hear people without hearts themselves sitting in judgment on me because I have too much experience to believe every selfish young man or woman a hero or a heroine. That common-place love which is professed every day is something widely different from the passion which only master minds can feel and describe. Take Shakespeare for instance. Who can read his works and not be convinced that he had experienced love. But he did not love his wife, an exceedingly common-place woman, older than himself, whom he married when a mere youth, full of romance, and unconscious of his own undeveloped powers. What right had such a woman to marry Shakespeare, or expect to engross the affections of such a man; of course he ran away from her—very properly."

Another arch look from Miss Lawrence, and a laugh from both girls ; but Mrs. Basil would not see it in a humourous light.

" You ought to be ashamed to advance such extraordinary and immoral opinions, Ernest."

" You exemplify the strictly virtuous and exemplary world, my mother, who will make no allowance for the failings of genius. It was a pity, if you like, for Shakespeare, or Milton, or other men of genius ever to marry the wives they did ; but as to living with them, trying to find nourishment and sympathy where none existed, who could expect it. Anne Hatheway's name has come down to posterity simply from being the wife of Shakespeare, but that he ever drew his inimitable heroines from her, or that her image occupied his mind when he wrote his sonnets, I can never believe. I love to read his Antony and Cleopatra and fancy it history, or at least surrender myself to the veil of romance that he has thrown over those two personages. Antony—the eloquent, ambitious, world-conquering, revelling, pleasure-loving

Antony, losing all for love ; Cleopatra—artful, cunning, inconstant, capricious, loving Antony, yet *ruining* him, great and almost amiable in her death "——

"Ernest, I wonder at you. What can you find to admire in a character like Cleopatra, who, although a queen, was neither more nor less than an—an abandoned woman ?"

Ernest threw himself back in his chair and laughed till the tears ran down his face.

"Well," he said at length, when he had somewhat recovered from his paroxysm of mirth, " that is certainly a view of the question which should have prevented Shakespeare from ever writing, or me from admiring the drama. My dear mother, you do amaze me, so because poor Cleopatra was never legally married, you will hear nothing said in her favour. Why persist in looking at this heroine of history only from the worst point of view. Consider her for once only as the Egyptian queen, the " serpent of old Nile", a woman born to magni-

ficence and power, whose blood coursed like lava through her veins. I fancy I see her at this moment, a woman after the Italian type, who, out of jealousy would aim a dagger at your heart one moment, and smother you with embraces the next; one who, considering her opportunities of working good and evil, might have been infinitely worse as well as better. Let us be carried away by the mighty magician as you open the volume and read the matchless tale, ' All for love or the world were lost.' Aye, is it not impressive," he continued with flashing eyes, " to find love represented no longer dwelling with sighing shepherds and lowly swains in retired valleys and Arcadian groves; but inspiring two beings, neither in the bloom or freshness of youth, both mighty, and rulers of men's destinies. Shakespeare has rightly conceived such characters as inspired by something more than mere caprice, or calculating interest. With what masterly sketches are we made to behold Queen Cleopatra sailing in triumphant state down the Cydnus, while " the city cast its people out upon her."

> " The wrangling queen,
> Whom everything becomes, to chide, to laugh,
> To weep.''

And that last scene where she emulates the death of Antony, who dies—

> " A Roman by a Roman, valiantly vanquished.''

where she says—

> " Show me my woman like a queen. Go fetch
> My best attires—I am again for Cydnus
> To meet Mark Antony.
> * * * *
> Give me my robe, put on my crown, I have
> Immortal longings in me.''

There is no knowing how long Ernest would have gone on multiplying quotations, had he not suddenly observed that Mrs. Basil had left the room; she had not waited to hear the defence of a character so notorious, so inexcusable, in her eyes, as Cleopatra Queen of Egypt.

Gradually the reserve which had characterized Miss Lawrence's manners began to wear off, and there is no knowing how far the amiability of character which each day unfolded might have influenced Ernest, had not the young lady in question been obliged to quit Mrs. Saunders' family at the end of a week to pay a visit to some other old friends to whom she was engaged, and in the time that intervened previous to her return, Ernest had made the acquaintance of another young lady destined to have an important influence on his future career.

Baillie Flaccid was one of those characters termed highly respectable, that is, he had never been discovered in the act of stealing, or setting fire to a church, or any crime punishable by law. He did his duty faithfully to society by constantly attending to his own and family's interest, and slowly and surely adding field to field, and barn to barn, and by being seen regularly at Kirk on the Sabbath, himself in a blue coat and bright buttons, his wife and daughters with every imaginable article of finery which money could purchase or fashion permit them to wear. The three Misses Flaccid were, in their mother's and their own opinion, and that of all respectable people in

Y——, *model young ladies.* No expense was spared upon their education, and accordingly they possessed just that amount of shreds and patches of useless knowledge which go to form modern young ladies—and if a young lady's, education is finished when she can thrum on the piano, and execute strange combinations of apple-dumpling clouds and water-bewitched on Bristol board, if woman's mission consists in promenading during certain hours of the day, dressed up like popinjays, reading novels and waiting to be married, then indeed are the Misses Flaccid model young ladies.

On the first of the month, Ernest had received a very elegant little note containing Mrs. Flaccid's compliments, and requesting the pleasure of Mr. Basil's company to a *soirée* on the twenty-first, and accordingly, on the evening in question, Ernest found himself in the middle of a throng which at first rendered it a matter of difficulty to approach and pay his respects to his hostess.

CHAPTER II.

MRS. FLACCID AT HOME—ERNEST IS INTRODUCED TO
MISS CONSTANCE FAIRWEATHER.

" AND where is this Mr. Ernest Basil," said a young lady to her partner Mr. Pennywise Close, (of whom more anon) " Miss Lawrence said he would be here to-night. Pray point him out to me if you see him."

" Do you see *yon* young man," said Mr. Close speaking in a broad provincial dialect, which, to spare the reader and the printer, we will not repeat, " with the low forehead, and the hooked nose and all that hair about his face."

" What that handsome looking foreigner talking, to Miss Greenshields."

" That i'll be *him*," replied Mr. Close.

" How envious and illiberal to describe him as you have done. I think him the *best* looking man in the room. Now that he is talking so earnestly to Miss Greenshields, he looks quite picturesque. I like the foreign look which the moustache gives."

" Oh aye it may do very well for foreigners, though I don't see what business a poor devil of a portrait painter. has to wear one. Though I must say Mr. Basil's outlandish appearance does not belie him. I've heard Alec Flaccid who kens him weel say, that he can neither talk nor act like anybody else, that he never saw anybody sae odd. He's got the queerest crotchets in his head about politics and religion and the condition of the people. He says some things that are *just* ridiculous, that there ought to be *nae* poor, that all nations should be at peace, and I hae heard him myself disputing with the *wife* that has the bathing machines, and telling her that it would hae been better for Scotland if Calvin and John Knox had never been hard of."

" Pray go on" said the young lady with a mischievous smile "you cannot think how interested I am in hearing about this Mr. Basil who seems by your account to be quite an original."

Mr. Close continued. " I've *hard* Flaccid say he is a raal tiresome chap to be with aye *deaving* one with remarks on beauty, and *bletherin* away about this and *yon* fine effect. I've seen him standing looking out at sea, down by the bathing machines, for a great while without moving till one would almost fancy there was something to be seen. He's a powerful swimmer though, I've kenned him go out in rough weather farther than anybody else. Then Alec says he'll stand and admire the dirty little ragged bairns, and praise the shape of their legs and feet and say what fine studies they would make and mere nonsense of that sort, and as for beauty, Flaccid says he has no idea of it for he'll admire a poor beggar, or a red-armed country-lass when he winna look at a well-dressed woman. And that's all I know about him, he's an artist and from America, so no wonder he's sae odd."

" Oh I should so like to know him. Can you tell me anything more about Mr. Basil ?" said the young lady turning to Mr. Danvers a gentlemanly young man who had listened to Mr. Close's remarks with several signs of scorn and impatience.

" That I can, Miss Fairweather," said Danvers, " and my information, unlike Mr. Close's, is from personal knowledge of the party, and not picked up from hearsay and breach of confidence. Mr. Ernest Basil is the son of an officer in the army, both his parents are well recollected in Y———. That he has received an education, and that he possesses great original powers, half an hour in his company will testify. It is only within the last two or three years that he has taken to portrait painting as a profession, his previous leisure having been so well improved in reading and travelling, that I should not be at all surprised if we yet heard of him in the literary world. He has seen some of the wildest and most picturesque scenery, and resided in some of the chief cities of the New World. Those who know Mr. Basil as I have the pleasure of doing, will know an artist and a gentleman, and not a poor devil of a portrait painter, as Mr. Close so elegantly expressed it; and I have yet to learn that it is more disgraceful for a gentleman to make a living by so refined and beautiful an art, than to squander idly the means which the industry of others has accumulated."

Mr. Close, who was an idle man on six hundred a year, did not vouchsafe any reply to this rather pointed sentence.

In the meantime the subject of this attack and defence was engaged in a lively dialogue with a young lady whose bright eyes lent an additional piquancy to her conversation.

" I assure you it is true, Miss Greenshields, I was introduced to a young lady the other day whose beauty actually staggered me. I did not know that I was so susceptible to a *coup d'œil*, for I am no believer in love at first sight. I give you my word that the fair enslaver occupied my thoughts for a good half hour, and that as I walked down Grafton Street I did not look at one of the pretty girls I met, so engrossed was I with her image."

" Really, Mr. Basil, you must have been very deeply smitten, and the young lady would feel gratified if she knew the influence of her charms—half an-hour, did you say ?"

" For half an-hour consecutively did her image occupy my mind's eye, and occasionally at intervals during the rest of the day. Is not that pretty well for a general admirer. Really I am too much impressed with the fleeting nature of time to devote myself too long to one enslaver. Gracious, to think of spending the time in one flirtation which might have been devoted to twenty."

" Dear me, Mr. Basil, the atrocity of such principles is only equalled by your bare-faced effrontery in avowing them. So you confess you take an actual pleasure in breaking hearts?"

" Ah ! now you flatter me. Positively I fear I shall never have the honour of breaking a heart. I have often thought I should like to break a heart just as a trial that such things could be.   I have my doubts about such fractures.   No, I never had the presumption to be a lady-killer ; I merely go with the stream and try to please, perfectly ready to break my own heart or another's, equal to either fortune."

" I suppose you never intend to marry, Mr. Basil, since that would put a stop to your flirtations ?"

" Who can control his fate. Marriage seems an inevitable necessity.   But it would be a thousand pities to marry till one had exhausted his opportunities of flirtation. The proper time to marry is just that critical period when we can flirt no longer, and can settle down contentedly into the admired and admirers of unity—in a wife."

" Very well, Mr. Basil, I only wish your intended could hear you.   So you don't believe in constancy, and breaking hearts, and long engagements ?"

" Pretty and interesting things to read of, but———ah ! there is Miss Frigid, the diminutive refrigerator, as I call her, to distinguish her from Miss Zero, who is the magnificent refrigerator."

" Mr. Basil, how can you be so censorious, so wicked ?"

" What a refreshing coolness she dispenses around her, to be sure. Are you not sensible that the temperature is several degrees lower since she entered the room. She is better than an ice cream this warm weather."

" For shame !" said Miss Greenshields, looking very much pleased nevertheless.

" When she shook hands with me the other day, I felt a cold chill run up my arm to the elbow, and it has felt numbed ever since. Her manner is not at all diffident, which might imply some degree of latent caloric. She appears to glory in the shock of suspended animation she is about to inflict, and advances to shake hands with a studied and finished gravity redolent of the North Pole, which I rather like."

" How can you say so? I think her manner perfectly detestable."

" Oh, I feel grateful for the charming foil she makes to other young ladies of a different stamp, and you like frank, hearty people more than ever. After meeting her, Miss Gelid seems quite cordial."

" You are quite a philosopher to deduce such good results from a moral lump of ice."

" I think shaking hands gives you a good clue to character. What a variety of ways people have of performing the *manual* exercise. Some grasp your hand cordially, others squeeze it like a vice, some hold it in their own, others drop it as though it were a live coal, and others have got a most provoking way of putting their digits into yours, and then making no effort either to shake your hand or to withdraw their own. I am often inclined to inquire of such—now, sir, what am I to do with your hand now I have got it?"

" You are certainly very observing and very amusing, Mr. Basil, I have noticed these peculiarities, but never heard the subject so learnedly *handled* before."

" By the way," said Ernest, suddenly changing the topic of conversation, " I have a favour to ask. If you have a spare seat in your pew "——

" You are welcome at any time. Do you attend our chapel? I know you are not of the Romish communion."

" You are right, Miss Greenshields. But I am not so prejudiced as not to sympathise with all sincere worshippers."

" I am glad to hear you say so. But I am so accustomed to intolerance and prejudice on every side in this stronghold of fanaticism and bigotry, that I am surprised when I meet with anything like liberality or religious tolerance.'

" It was only the other day I heard," said Ernest, " that some impertinent zealot was actually standing at the entrance of your chapel thrusting *Free Church* pamphlets into the hands of the congregation as they went in. I could not have believed that the spirit of intolerance was so rife in the Free Church."

" Oh ! that is nothing, I assure you," said Miss Greenshields, " I have been told to my face that I worshipped idols, and that my religion was a lot of mummery."

" It appears to me," said Ernest, " that the Free Church would make a worse use of power than (excuse me) the Popes ever did. You will pardon me for speaking frankly of the Romish religion, because the church of the present is not the church of the past ; but the Papal power never in its worst days warred against the art of refinement and knowledge, save where they tended directly to interfere with ecclesiastical authority. I have witnessed the celebration of high mass in the imposing cathedral of Montreal, where ten thousand worshippers can kneel, as well as the procession of the Féte Dieu, and nowhere, perhaps, with

the exception of Rome itself, is the worship of
your church calculated to make a stronger impression upon an ardent and refined imagination, for it is to the minds of the intelligent
rather than the ignorant, that the poetry of
Roman worship more particularly appeals. It
is the opinion of the Roman Church that the
reverence and honour due to the Creator should
tax all the gifts and powers of men, His creatures. Hence she summons man's genius in
the several departments of painting, architecture, sculpture, and music; all unite in her
service, not in the vain idea that the creature can
offer anything sufficiently worthy to the Creator,
but that through the ministry of these arts, which
cherish lofty and sublime thoughts tending
to soften and humanise the soul, we may come
before our Maker in the most exalted frame of
mind. The Redeemer looks down upon the
kneeling multitudes, the solemn peal of the
organ, vocal and instrumental harmony blend
with the confession and supplication of sinners,
and while the censers send forth the fragrant

incense, the officiating priest clothed in purple
and gold and fine linen, like the Levite of old,
performs the solemn rite in token of expiation
of sins by the blood of the Saviour. And this
grand and pathetic ritual, which, to those who
comprehend its mysterious intent, must seem
beautiful, even independently of belief, is
termed mummery by the ignorant sectarian,
priding himself on his own narrow prejudices,
unable to extend his glance beyond his own
meagre forms, into anything possessing beauty
and sublimity. Such an one may well scoff
and jeer at a worship so different from his own
bald, bare worship. And yet, in spite of this
holy horror of fanaticism, superstition, and
idolatry, your sectarian is not the less a fanatic
—not the less an idol worshipper, after a different fashion. Enter the Free Church—there
is no architecture, no sculpture, no paintings,
no organ, no incense, no altar, no effigy of
saint or apostle, but there is an idol, nevertheless ; and where will you find him ?—in the

pulpit—it is the preacher. Let them congratulate themselves as they will in having abjured the cross because they choose to consider it as a type of Popery—let them refuse to bend the knee or the head when they pray, or at the name of Jesus, and then find them hanging inconsistently on the words of a frail mortal like themselves, listening to his inventive powers instead of praying; and drinking in with greedy ears his uncouth barbarous exposition of his Maker's ways, his offensively familiar method of speaking of the Deity, and then answer the question—which is the idol worshipper? The preacher is more a god to the Free Church congregation than the crucifix to the Papist. It is he they talk of when they leave the kirk busrting with pride of the preacher's eloquence—the number of heads into which he divides his sermon—the way he stuck to his text—and the setting down he gave the Catholics or some other body of fellow Christians. Can the Free Church with any consistency attack Rome for her intolerance and bigotry? Would the Free Church have preserved to us the arts and sciences which Rome did. A pretty mistress of learning and protectoress of knowledge and art during the dark ages the Free Church would have made. Look at her churches and worship in the nineteenth century, alike barren of beauty— look at the principles she openly advocates, intolerance and fanaticism, and contempt of cultivation and refinement ;—her clergymen drawn from the humbler classes, and generally possessing neither talent, liberality, nor manners—look at the results of Free Church teaching in the hypocrisy which she sows broadcast over society, more particularly in the mischievous training of the young, and in the specious attention to the outward forms of devotion and puritanical observance of the Sabbath, a mere cloak to hide immorality, as the statistics of vice in the great cities of Scotland prove. Let the Free Church look at home, and she will find the very faults with which she charges the Roman church, viz., a narrowing in of the faculties of the mind by an artificial system of religion. Is this church which is studiously labouring to disconnect art, beauty, and intellect from the worship of the Most High, the fitting representative of a great enlightened country like Scotland in the nineteenth century. Is she not a precocious child who improves on the errors of a parent, who expelled one of her clergy for *the crime of genius?* Home, the author of Douglas. There is little fear, however, of a Free Church clergyman being expelled for a similar crime, for where is there one capable of writing a tragedy? There is some excuse for the errors of the church of Rome as the offspring and growth of the dark ages. They have the protecting influence of age and tradition to hallow and support them. The narrow prejudices of the Free Church of Scotland have no such excuse, they are the results of profound ponderings

of past experience, grafted on modern enlightenment, practically staying the progress
of intelligence, the perception of truth and
beauty towards the northern extremity of Great
Britain."

"Well done, Mr. Basil," exclaimed Miss
Greenshields, who had listened attentively,
" you are certainly coming over to us."

" There you are mistaken Miss Greenshields,"
replied Ernest, delighted at having found
so good a listener and embued with the spirit of
argument. " Every religion has its share of
excellence, and I cannot help doing justice to
truth and beauty wherever I find it, but as I am
speaking so frankly, I need not hesitate to say
that I know no one farther from Rome than
myself. The very impartiality which renders
me so alive to the beauties of your religion
makes me equally clear sighted to its errors.
The unthinking zealot is one day a Protestant,
another a Catholic shifting with every wind of
doctrine according as he meets with intellect

more subtle than his own. He may be *converted* though he never can *convert*, but the intelligent philosopher despises alike hypocrisy and priestcraft whether practised by Protestant, Presbyterian or Papist. Such a one places virtue and religion in actions not in professions and can lift his thoughts to his maker either in the temple raised by man or under the illimitable arch of Heaven, the dome of the Almighty architect. His mind soars above the distinctions of a surplice or a Geneva gown or the important question which occupies *bishops, whether candles should be lighted or unlighted on the altar*, and he regards with pitying wonder the multitudes of rational beings calling themselves men not school boys who actually occupy their minds with such trifles and call it *religion*. Miss Greenshields are you now convinced that I am not coming over to Rome. Have you ever read, ' Priests, Women, and Families ?' "

" No indeed and I never will either, for Father Petrie says it is a very bad book. I give you up Mr. Basil."

" For an obstinate heretic" said Basil with a
laugh, " but what a charming polka. Have
you any scruples of conscience in dancing
with me."

" None whatever," said Miss Greenshields,
and away they went a beautiful example of ball-
room tolerance.

Miss Constance Fairweather, the young lady
who had made enquiries respecting Ernest,
already recorded, had overheard the greater
part of the dialogue between him and Miss
Greenshields under cover of a flirtation which
she had been carrying on with Mr. Flaccid Junr.

" Oh here is your beau ideal" exclaimed
Flaccid as Ernest passed after leading Miss
Greenshields to a seat. " I will introduce you,"
and in a moment without any previous inti-
mation to Ernest, the talismanic words had been
pronounced which converted two strangers into
acquaintances, and Mr. Alec Flaccid, apparently very well satisfied with his able diplomacy,
pulled up his collar, looked at his boots, and

then strutted away leaving Ernest to *improve the opportunity* or not as he chose. Ernest's first impulse had been to pass on ; but a glimpse of Miss Fairweather showed him such a handsome young lady, that almost before he was conscious, he had asked and secured her hand for the next quadrille. Leaving them then to break the ice of first acquaintance, we shall endeavour to furnish a faint sketch of the young lady who is to ocupy rather a prominent part in our forthcoming pages.

Miss Constance Fairweather, had been left an orphan at a very early age, and was now believed to be wholly dependent upon an uncle in India, who was reputed to be very wealthy, but whether she was to be his heiress or not was not decided upon by the gossips of Y——, who kindly interested themselves in their neighbour's affairs. But as Miss Becky Blab discreetly remarked, " a' things canna be known and it was best to be on the *ceevil* side ony waie." So whenever her uncle happened to be in Y——,

Miss Fairweather was overwhelmed with invitations, and attentions from people who seemed to forget her existence at his departure. At present she divided her time between her grandmother at Bonner and Y——, where she was under the temporary guardianship of a Mrs. Grainger.

Miss Fairweather possessed one of those brilliant red and white complexions, which it is difficult to class under the head of blonde or brunette, though perhaps it inclined to the latter. Her eyes were a dark blue, her mouth neither large nor small but finely formed, her hair of dark brown and luxuriant, formed a striking feature in her style of beauty. It possessed such a decided curl that it formed a regular line of beauty on her alabaster brow, and then took its wilful way disdaining curb or fillet and fell in long graceful ringlets down to her very waist. Her figure was large, finely formed; her movements full of grace and elasticity; as for her character, we leave that to develope itself.

" Do for goodness sake Mr. Basil go back to

your beautiful partner," said Miss Greenshields at a later hour in the evening. " She will stare her eyes out if you don't, you seem to have made quite a conquest already. Who is she."

" That is more than I can tell you," said Ernest " for although I have been dancing with her, my memory for names is so bad that I have forgotten hers already: however, Flaccid will tell you, he knows all about her."

" She is very pretty," said Miss Greenshields, " don't you think so ?"

" Oh she's well enough," said Ernest, who was fond of getting one woman's opinion of another.

" Is that all you can say, and yet you are an artist and profess to have a taste in beauty. To my mind she is perfect *in her way*." And Miss Greenshields began to grow quite eloquent in praise of Miss Fairweather's nose, mouth and eyes.

" Upon my word Miss Greenshields," said Ernest, bending a look of great admiration in the direction of Miss Fairweather, " you are right, she is very beautiful. I see it now, the fact was I found her conversation so pleasant, that I had not time to think of her looks; but as you say, she is charming. What a superb neck, what an elegant contour, and her movements are grace itself."

" Yes," said Miss Greenshields, with a good deal less enthusiasm than before in her tone. " She has, as you say a *nice* figure, but—don't you think her waist is rather large, and I must say I cannot extend my admiration to her taste in dress. That sombre velvet is anything but becoming to her, and I think now that I look at her face again, that her upper lip is a little too short; but perhaps she sits with her mouth open on purpose to show her teeth, which seem tolerable from here."

Reader have you never observed how one pretty woman will run on in praise of another until you put in your oar and begin to praise too. The reason is obvious; Miss A. in praising

Miss B. is displaying the magnanimity and disinterestedness of her own character, and there is a pleasing hope at bottom, that the listener may be thinking how good, and kind, and charitable, Miss A. is, rather than of the beautiful Miss B.

CHAPTER III.

ALEC. FLACCID, as he was generally called,
(son of Baillie Flaccid), had no peculiarity of
character at all discernible beyond a remarkable fondness for acquiring and detailing news,
a faculty in which he surpassed even Miss Becky
Blab, or any lady of certain or uncertain age.
No sooner had this charming youth heard anything than he became perfectly restless and
uneasy until he had told it to the next person
he met, without the least regard to the mischief
which might ensue from his tattling, and as
none of his stories ever lost in the repetition,

it may be supposed that Master Alec. was at the bottom of a good many misunderstandings and interruptions of friendships. When Ernest had discovered this peculiarity in Mr. Flaccid, that he could keep nothing to himself, but was a sort of human magpie, who might be made the unconscious instrument either of good or evil, he endeavoured to turn it to account by only uttering in Flaccid's presence such sentiments as were calculated for the widest circulation. If for instance, he wished anything to reach a person's ears, he had only to tell it to Flaccid in confidence, and that young gentleman seldom slept until he had put it in train to reach the party. As Ernest remarked, he was a surer medium of communication than the town crier, who was old and toothless, and had not besides the advantage of moving in the same circles which Flaccid frequented. By this method he flattered himself that he had derived as much good and as little injury from Flaccid as possible ; yet, as it was, he had some difficulty to refrain from telling him his mind, when

he found proof of his meddling in his affairs. To
quarrel with him outright would have been un-
safe as long as he remained within the sphere
of his michief-making powers. For this reason
Ernest bore with him, mentally determining to
have a day of reckoning for any serious injury
that Flaccid's tale-bearing might effect, and
for the boredom which he had already inflicted.

" And what does Miss Fairweather think of
me ?" said Ernest to Flaccid, as they walked
down Grafton Street together a few days after
the party.

" Oh she's delighted with you, she would
have it at first you were a foreigner."

" Indeed," said Ernest, who often amused himself with pumping Flaccid, but who had never
found any subject so interesting as the present
to talk about with him. " Every new acquaintance is a blessing now ; besides, Miss Fairweather interests me, she's so like a young
lady I knew in New York. What makes you
stare so ?"

"A young lady in New York!" said Flaccid, "you're joking surely."

"What do you mean, why should I be joking, why shouldn't Miss Fairweather be like a young lady I knew in New York?"

"Why, I thought there were no young ladies in America."

"You thought," said Ernest, hardly disguising his contempt. "What did you think there were there then?"

"Why nothing but Factory girls and women of that sort."

"I can tell you, if you were to see an American factory girl, such as I have seen at Lowell, near Boston, who plays on a piano, and writes articles in a magazine, you might think there might be young ladies even in America. But where does Miss Fairweather live? Tell me all about her there's a good fellow."

"She lives with Mrs. Grainger, a very strict Free-Church lady——"

"Not much chance of making acquaintance in that quarter, eh?"

" No, she's like the rest of them in this blessed place——"

" Looks upon a young lady left in her charge as a sort of prisoner, a valuable moveable, never to be let out of sight if possible ?"

" Exactly so, we aye call her Mrs. Jellaby, because she minds a' body's business but her own," said Flaccid, describing his own character and Mrs. Grainger's at the same time.

" One would think that young ladies were particularly liable to be run away with by the gallant gay Lothario's of Y——, and yet I don't know that an elopement is a very common occurrence."

" Mrs. Grainger is only her temporary guardian till her uncle the nabob returns from India."

" An heiress, so much the better ; really I begin to take quite a violent interest in this Miss Fairweather. I never knew an heiress with ten thousand pounds who was not a most amiable girl."

" Aye, indeed," said Flaccid, who had not

the most remote idea of a joke. " Mind though,
I'm na sure she's an heiress."

" Heiress or not it's no matter; I'm going
to love her for her own sake."

" She'll be a bonnie lassie, though she's no
overly civil. She told Bella that I was a mere
boy the other night. Boy indeed, I am a year
older than she is. I'm thinking you won't
care for her when you know her as well as
I do."

" I'd like to judge for myself, and I reckon
upon your help Flaccid in doing all you can to
further our acquaintance. I always introduce
you to the pretty girls I know. Come along
and point out the house to me. I forget the
number."

" Well you do appear in earnest."

" How can I be anything else but *Ernest*."

" Well, I can tell you for your comfort, that
Miss Fairweather and my sisters are very inti-
mate, and the first time she is at our house
I'll let you know."

" Thank you, how can I show my gratitude ?

Name any particular beauty I happen to know
and you don't."

" Well, you promissed long ago to introduce
me to Miss Blair."

" Consider yourself introduced already."

" Well, but I can't till it's done. At least
she wouldn't speak to me if I bowed to her, so
what good would it do me."

" It shall de done the very first opportunity.
Miss Blair will be at a small party which my
mother intends to give in a fortnight, and in
the mean time I will give her such a character
of you that she shall love you at first sight."

" And now I think of it, there's that new
beauty from the country, Miss Lawrence, who
was staying at your home, and is now at Mrs.
Borem's."

" What, you want to destroy my happiness
there also. See what a disinterested fellow I
am. I pointed you out to her the other day as
you passed and said a word in your favour.
Ah that's the house is it. Now I wouldn't
stare at the window for the world, but I'll con-

trive to find out if she's there. This is the dodge you see; I look behind very anxious to discover if I know that person coming along the road, and then I bring myself round gradually with a thoughtful unconscious look at the opposite houses. I declare somebody has come to the window—I do believe it is she. Tell me quick Alec.; I daren't take another look."

" Aye, it's *her*," said Alec.

" How I envy you the privilege of calling at that house," said the impetuous Ernest, " but I'll tell you what it is; couldn't you bring Miss Fairweather with your sisters to call on my mother, and then my mother can ask you all together to come to our little *soirée*." This plan was fully discussed and decided upon, and Ernest parted with Flaccid, thinking him not such a bad fellow after all, and feeling that for his introduction to Miss Fairweather alone, he owed him a debt of gratitude. Several times in the interval between this and the evening appropriated for Mrs. Basil's party, Ernest met Miss Fairweather, and each time received a most gracious bow, and once when he stopped and spoke to her, her manner was so remarkably cordial, that he felt sure that Flaccid must have made her acquainted with the greater part of what he had said concerning her. He always praised Miss Fairweather to Flacid now whenever he met him, and he certainly found it no very hard task to do so, and as he generally concluded with begging Flaccid not to tell her what he had said, he had no doubt whatever that every word reached her ears, which was the fact.

The innocent little scheme turned out perfectly successful. The ladies came, visited Mr. Basil's studio, and were invited by Mrs. Basil to come on a certain evening. Miss Fairweather begged to be allowed to accept conditionally, " she feared she was engaged for that evening both to a dinner and an evening party. She could not get off the dinner party, but she thought she might the other—she would try." The evening came, all were assembled with the exception of Miss Fairweather. Never had the Misses Flaccid appeared more insipid to Ernest, as he danced with one after the other, and wished most devoutly that the evening was at an end.   At ten o'clock, Miss Fairweather made her appearance, and then, indeed, things wore a different appearance to Mr. Basil. The sudden brightening up of his manner, and abrupt change from dullness to loquacity, did not escape the observation of the elder Miss Flaccid, and did not pass without a remark.

" Why, Mr. Basil, how lively you seem all at once."

" I am afraid you have found me a very dull partner hitherto, Miss Flaccid, but the fact is I have been suffering all the evening from a violent tooth-ache, which has left me within the last five minutes."

" Tooth-ache ?—I thought you said the head-ache before.   Well, I thought you seemed relieved all at once.   I noticed it just when Miss Fairweather entered the room. What an odd coincidence that the tooth-ache or the head-ache should leave you just at that moment."

"Very odd," said Ernest, drily, as the quadrille came to an end, and he hastened to pay his respects to Miss Fairweather.

Already in his short acquaintance with Miss Fairweather Ernest thought he had discovered symptoms of a mind worthy of her personal attractions. There had been as yet, to be sure, little opportunity for learning the depth of Miss Fairweather's sentiments, but he felt certain that she possessed both cultivation and feeling from the frankness with which she inspired him. There are some people who win our confidence at once—there is a congeniality of spirit which makes itself known at a glance. While with the Misses Flaccid and others, Ernest never got beyond the most common and superficial topics—" mere bald disjointed chat ;" but before he had been speaking to Miss Fairweather five minutes, they seemed somehow to be old acquaintances.

"Am I right in believing that it was a glimpse of Miss Fairweather's angelic form that I caught sight of on Thursday, when I passed your house? I am sure you will acquit me of staring, but I could not resist just one look."

"Oh! I saw you and forgave you; but your impudence did not pass scot free. Some one else saw you too, and made the remark, looking very hard at poor me—'I suppose Mr. Basil wants a subject for a picture.'"

"And who was my fair enemy?"

"Her name is Legion. She is only one among numerous beings who cannot, by any possibility, say a good-natured thing."

"It has often struck me that the condition of the young ladies here was anything but enviable. They seem all to live in dread of some exceedingly kind elderly maiden ladies voluntarily appoint themselves to an office who which has not been legally renewed since the days of ancient Rome. *Censores morum.* How indebted the *young* young ladies must feel to these *old* young ladies for thus watching over the conduct of the rising generation. Yet it cannot be denied that it produces want of frankness. I am honoured by an introduction to a young lady, I dance with her, and do my poor best to make myself agreeable. And the next day she cuts me downright, or gives me a cold freezing bow, and at the end of six months we have made no further progress towards acquaintance than at the close of the first evening. It must be confessed that it takes some time to get accustomed to such manners. From the cold greetings which take place in the market place, one would imagine that the men were monks and women nuns, vowed to eternal celibacy. What surprises a stranger is that any marriages ever do take place."

" I don't think any ever do," said Miss Fairweather, laughing.

" Alas, then, who are we to thank for this sad state of things but the voluntary censors before alluded to? I have heard that some

young ladies are beginning to have moral scruples about dancing the polka. It makes one
ask—

Can such things be,
And overcome us, like a summer's cloud,
Without our special wonder ?

There is a young lady here from Paris, now residing with some Free Church family in Y——.
I have heard, but I will not vouch for it, that
she has actually supported two months of
gaiety and dissipation of life in Y——. Poor
thing, I met her the other day guarded by two
solemn females. There seemed to be still
some shadow of former mirth lingering beneath the mask of dullness and propriety to
which she had been broken in. It is gratifying to learn, however, that the time of her
pennance approaches a close. I find it difficult
to live in Y—— after New York. What must
it be after Paris? I took up a number of the
Tableau de Paris the other day, and it made
me quite melancholy to think of vegetating
here while there were such places as Paris,
Rome, Florence, and Venice unvisited."

" You must not forget, Mr. Basil, that women have a thousand resources in the very
weakness of their minds which are denied to
men. We can shop, and crozier, and spend
hours talking about the shape of a collar or
the colour of a ribbon. You speak much
more gently of Y—— than you feel. I know
what strangers think of it. I could read your
sentiments, only in compliment to my patriotic
prejudices, you would not confirm them if I
should give them utterance."

" My dear Miss Fairweather, I am tempted
to take you at your word; the slightest attempt to analyze my thoughts or my sympathies with my feelings, is now so rare to me,
that I—but you have travelled, you have lived
abroad on the continent, that makes the bond
between us."

" To one like you," continued Miss Fairweather, " the prospect of a continued residence in Y—— must be dreadful. Corinna
was not moie wretched than you would be were
your life in Y—— anything but a mere epi-

sode, to make the past more pleasing, the fu
turemore engaging. Even I, a woman, would almost as lieve suffer bodily as mental captivity, but
to a man, whose happiness consists in action, to
have no friend, no sympathy, to be compelled
to turn for ever within for consolation, and confined by the thorny hedge of earth-born maxims
amid a religious boasting, piety arrogating
community, virtually deaf to ideas which have
not the main chance stamped upon them. Is
it not thus you think of Y——? I know you
hate it."

"Lately I have begun to think Y—— much
pleasanter."

"I knew you were too gallant to give me
a plump yes. But let us be a little less *dans
le serieux*, during this quadrille, or I don't
know what Miss Flaccid will think of us. Pray
why did you not bow to me to-day when you
met me with Miss Flaccid and Miss Hilaire?"

"Not bow to you? Why I am sure I made
a most decided and comprehensive inclination."

" Still you did not bow to *me*," said Miss Fairweather, in a serious tone.

" You would not have had me give three distinct nods, like a Chinese mandarin. If you could have read my thoughts, you would have known that I was most anxious to turn and walk with you. But I was afraid you would think me officious on our short acquaintance. Miss Hilaire I know very well. She is always cheerful, and we are good friends."

" Oh, yes, and you can bow to her and not to me."

" Spare my feelings, recollect I am from the back woods of America. How should I know how to bow correctly ?"

" You shan't turn the tables upon me. The back woods indeed—you a poet and an artist."

" Do not quiz me quite so openly. When did I give myself out for a poet ?"

" Poetry and painting generally go together. At least you are an author. You will not deny that when I have read your articles in magazines."

" In a very small way as yet—and as for
poetry I never attempt it but on very particular occasions. I shall not forget two occasions of my writing in albums, on account of
the very different succcess which my poetical
effusions received. In the first instance, the
lady actually shed tears over the affecting
verses I wrote. In the latter, the young lady
received the album from my hand, laid it on
the drawing-room table, and thanked me for
my trouble without reading my lines. I have
never written in an album since."

" So you confess to have written poetry
moving enough to cause a lady's tears to flow."

" You would make me vain if I thought you
were not quizzing."

" Quizzing, indeed !"

" What else can I imagine ?—a poor portrait painter, without the patronage even of the
provincial town in which I reside—I, who every
day feel bitterly that I have yet done nothing
to fulfil the over sanguine expectations of par-

tial friends, or to make the world believe in me."

"Mr. Basil," interrupted Miss Fairweather, " I see you are speaking from your heart, and I protest against such an unfair judgment of yourself. Your self depreciation of what you have done, and how many young men at your age have done much less, proves what you are capable of achieving. Whether in literature or in art, I feel convinced that you will fulfil the most sanguine expectations of your well-wishers."

There was an air of sincerity in Miss Fairweather's speech which made it go to his heart.

" Such language from you," he said, in a low voice, " awakes all my slumbering incentives to ambition. There are times when the dreary monotonous life I lead here has made my art seem worthless, and the future cheerless."

" But there are two sides to every question. It is but fair that you should know what others think of you. It will not make *you* vain."

"I wish you could always appear before me like my good angel to chase away the sad and gloomy reflections which sometimes beset me. It is better to be too sanguine than too despairing. We are happy, and at least we work while we are *hoping*."

"Imagine my presence, then, at such times," said Miss Fairweather, with a bewitching smile. "With your powers of fancy it would not be difficult."

"Delightful as the occupation will be, it will fall far short of the reality."

Whether by accident or by a little manœuvering we cannot undertake to say, but it is a fact that Ernest escorted Miss Fairweather home that evening. A servant had arrived for that purpose from Mrs. Grainger's about an hour after Miss Fairweather made her appearance at Mrs. Basil's. But as the Misses Flaccid intended to walk home, why not all go together?

Ernest was busy at his easel one day not long after this evening, when Mrs. Basil entered the studio with two young ladies. The first, as Ernest saw with keen delight, was Miss Fairweather, behind her came the blushing Miss Lawrence.

· " Mr. Basil," said Miss Fairweather, when the first greetings were over, " how sly you were about your acquaintance with my friend, Miss Lawrence, who, I find, has actually been living here, and you have been sketching her likeness, and making love to her, perhaps "—

" Oh l Constance," interrupted Miss Lawrence, hastily, and afterwards blushing at her own vehemence, " how can you say such things ?"

The beauty of these two young ladies was so dissimilar in character, that neither had any cause to fear rivalry from the other. They served rather mutually to set off one another to the best advantage.

Miss Fairweather was a dashing beauty, all sparkle and vivacity—one of those girls who take our hearts by storm, as it were.

Elinor Lawrence resembled some transcendant picture or statue which escapes general notice, and only attracts the *idolatry* of a connoisseur. The one was a brilliant fantasia which arrests the listener's attention—the other the soft and melting strain of sacred music, which, heard by one attuned to receive it, haunts the heart for ever. The one was the gaudy tulip of the parterre—the other the beauteous lily under the shadow of the rock.

Need we pursue our similes further. In plain prose let us say that Miss Fairweather's ease and sprightliness of manner gave her an advantage in general company over the quiet and demure Miss Lawrence, in spite of the greater personal attractions which an impartial observer would have awarded as the latters share. At first sight you would have called Miss Lawrence the most beautiful, Miss Fairweather the most engaging.

Miss Fairweather would not be satisfied till Mr. Basil had produced some of his sketches of Miss Lawrence, which were pronounced like, but not beautiful enough.

" And now show me some of Miss Lawrence's sketches," said Miss Fairweather.

Ernest looked astonished. " Do you draw ?" he asked, turning to Miss Lawrence.

" And Miss Lawrence has lived in the same house with you a week and yet you never found that out. Why Elinor how deceitful you are," said Miss Fairweather laughing, " not to have told Mr. Basil you could draw."

" Mr. Basil never asked me," said Miss Lawrence, with *naïveté.*

" I thought two artists would have found one another out. Why she paints, Mr. Basil, beautifully. Landscapes, heads, everything. There Elinor, take up the brush and finish that little head Mr. Basil is painting."

" Is it possible," exclaimed Mr. Basil, " that you conceal such a talent ? Let me second Miss Fairweather's request. Imitate the artists of antiquity who always left behind them some token of their visits to one another. Leave me some tangible proof that you and Miss Fairweather have been really here and that it is not a dream of an angel's visit."

" I'll tell you what," said the animated Miss Fairweather, " you shall sketch Mr. Basil. Mr. Basil, I order you to sit still in the most picturesque attitude you can assume until Miss Lawrence has done with you."

" Then I shall fall down on my knees like a despairing lover," said Ernest who seemed very much inclined to suit the action to the word. Suppose we make a group. Miss Lawrence, couldn't you put Miss Fairweather into the picture ?" After a good deal of badinage, Ernest sat down with his head perked up in the air, while Miss Lawrence took up the brush, but her sitter certainly tried her patience considerably, as he hardly ceased talking for a moment while his sallies from time to time caused a good deal of laughter, not tending to the advance of the painting. At the end of an hour and a half, Miss Lawrence had produced an unfinished, but clever little sketch of Ernest's head, upon which many encomiums were lavished by Miss Fairweather and Ernest.

"I shall treasure this, believe me, Miss Lawrence. I shall have no occasion now to bite my thumb like the sleeper awakened, to know whether this is not a dream."

Before the young ladies took their departure, Mrs. Basil invited them to drink tea and attend a concert afterwards with herself and Ernest on the following evening.

As soon as they were in the street, the young ladies began talking about Mr. Basil as was very natural under the circumstances.

"Well, what do you think of him Elinor you have known him longer than me?"

"Longer but not more intimately. One would think you were quite old friends to hear you talk. Mr. Basil never took half the pains to make himself agreeable to me as he does to you."

"Well Elinor, don't evade the question," said Constance, not without a secret exultation at Miss Lawrence's admission, " what do you think of him ?"

" I think he likes to please others and make them fond of him, but that he will be very difficult to please himself."

" Exactly my opinion Elinor. only differently expressed ; for I thought him a delightful fellow and a desperate flirt."

CHAPTER IV.

How long Ernest might have gone on cultivating Miss Fairweather's acquaintance under
the present exciting difficulties (for Mrs.
Grainger had never called as he expected she
would have done on his mother), it is impossible
to say, but for one of those chance occurrences
which, threatening to break off all acquaintance,
had the effect of more closely cementing it.

At an hour in the afternoon earlier than they
were expected to tea, both young ladies called
and Ernest was both surprised and mortified to
hear Miss Fairweather excuse herself from the

engagement she had made on the previous day, without assigning (in his opinion) any adequate cause, for they were going to the concert with Alec Flaccid and some of his sisters. Miss Fairweather did say something about not being able to quit home, owing to Mrs. Grainger's absence, till a certain hour; but Ernest's pride had taken fire, and was at no particular pains to conceal his opinion of conduct so *nonchalante* as Miss Fairweather's appeared to be. Mrs. Basil did not appear to mind it and gave the ladies a cordial invitation for the next disengaged evening, which happened to be Friday, but Ernest did not second it and only expressed a cold regret " that Miss Fairweather should think fit to permit a subsequent engagement to interfere with a previous one."

" You will not care to go to the concert now Ernest," said his mother. But in this she was mistaken. Mr. Basil was just enough in love with Miss Fairweather to take a pleasure in resenting her conduct and he determined to go to the concert to pique her if possible. He could not avoid noticing her and Miss Lawrence when he entered and replied with a stately bow to their recognition.

Why did Mr. Basil find so much to say that evening to his next door neighbour, Miss Greenshields. Why did he raise his voice in expressing his admiration of the principal singer, a tall dark Italian. Why did he smile and look so particularly pleased and engrossed in his *tête-à-tête*, when Miss Fairweather turned her head from Mr. Flaccid, who did not appear to be making himself very agreeable. And why did he salute Miss Fairweather with such a cold, " I hope you have been amused," at the expiration of the concert.

The whole of the next day, Wednesday, he still felt indignant. He thought it very probable that his acquaintance with Miss Fairweather was at an end, and " he could not *help it if* it was." The next day his insulted majesty began to be somewhat appeased: his heart began to soften and relent. After all it would be a pity to lose such a pleasant acquaintance for such a trifle, and Friday was spent in one continued conflict between hope and fear, as to whether they would accept his mother's invitation for that evening.

Six o'clock struck and Mrs. Basil and her son sat one on each side of the table with the tea-tray between them. The calmness of Ernest's voice offered no clue to the disappointment of his mind as he said—

" Depend upon it my mother they will not come. They have taken offence in their turn, and my acquaintance with Miss Fairweather is at an end." Just then the door-bell rang : a moment of cruel suspense intervened, and Ernest was astonished at his own feelings of delight when he recognized Miss Fairweather's voice. How would she meet him, would she be angry or reserved, would she quiz or scold him ?

Both young ladies (how beautiful they seemed on that evening to Ernest) met his profferred hand with their usual frankness. There seemed to be a tacit agreement that no explanation was required, and that they were to be all as good friends as ever. They sat down to tea quite a merry party, Ernest and Miss Fairweather seeming to vie with one another which could be in the highest spirits. Long afterwards did he remember that happy evening, with its rational conversation and music.

" Do you know, I begin to think, Mr. Basil, that a share of romance is not such an unfortunate component of our characters as the worldlings would make us believe. What a dreary thing it would be if we could not take refuge sometimes from a world of propriety and money-making, in fairy-land. Those dreadful matter-of-fact people, what have they to fall back upon in the hour of disappointment when they discover that their world of reality is at an end, and that *they* perhaps are the most foolish of dreamers ? I am beginning to think, and some day shall dare to tell Mrs. Grainger that I glory in a heart, and would rather be Undine with a soul than Undine without."

" You have read that most charming legend.
The allegory is so beautifully and richly
clothed, that many, I fancy, miss the exquisite moral."

" Pray give us your idea of it, Mr. Basil,"
said Miss Lawrence.

" It is intended to show what poor clods we
are until love has awakened a soul within us,
and that until we are thus awakened to the
responsibility of loving another, our views are
selfish, thoughtless, and temporal."

" True," said Miss Lawrence, " you have
read it I see to purpose."

" I confess," said Miss Fairweather, " that I
did not take such a deep view of it when I first
read it, for, as you say, the mind is so engrossed and filled up with the beauty of the
story, that we are apt to forget the deep-hidden
meaning."

" Pray Miss Fairweather," said Mrs. Basil,
" favour us with a little music," a request
which was warmly seconded by Ernest, and
Miss Fairweather sat down to the piano.   She

had received her musical education in Germany, and had indeed profited by her ample opportunities.   What was there she could not play, from the simplest ballad up to the most transcendental of operas? If there is a heaven upon earth, it is in youth listening to an accomplished young lady playing and singing, thus bringing *music* home to the Lares and Penates, where you can surrender yourself untrammelled by an audience to the spell of enchantment.   How inexpressibly grateful to the listener is that trill, those few skilfully touched notes, bursting with such pleasant abruptness upon the ear, and preparing it for the delicious harmony which is to follow.

Are young ladies aware, but of course they *are not*, to what advantage they display themselves while thus engaged?   While their fingers are wandering over the keys, and their figures sway gently to and fro in acknowledgement of the measured cadence with a delightful *abandon* which makes itself felt in its results upon young gentlemen's hearts, while

from the parted lips pours forth the gushing
melody, which you (if a masculine reader)
would only like to stop in one way—rising,
swelling into notes of ravishing sweetness,
which give delight, but we cannot say " hurt
not," for they are apt to leave severe pains in
young gentlemen's hearts. Do young ladies
ever think at such times, but of course *they
don't*, what delightful reveries in which they
mingle and form the principal figure, (in artist's
phrase) may be passing through the minds of
sundry young bachelors, more especially he
who occupies the most dangerous position of
any, the wight who stands behind the syren
and turns over the leaves. Really if we had
windows in our breasts, as some remarkably
odd and original heathen suggested, it might
be very inconvenient to have our thoughts
laid open to general inspection at such times.

Like all imaginative men, Ernest was keenly
alive to the effects of music, and somehow
Miss Fairweather's singing stirred the inmost
depths of his soul. All the hackneyed terms

of praise seemed insufficient and inadequate
to describe the gloriously natural triumph of
her voice—no affected pauses, no studied
shakes, art was quite forgotten in the gush
of melody which swept on with passionate
earnestness as though the singer was impro-
vising both music and words.　The listener
forgot to murmur occasionally, " beautiful,"
" very sweet," and similar compliments.　There
was no hurrying to request another song, and
Miss Fairweather was quite satisfied that it
should be so, she desired no more flattering
tribute than silence, and now and then the tear
trickling down the cheek.　How strange ! she
sang songs which he had not heard for years—
songs which removed a curtain from events and
scenes long gone by, and brought them back
clear and distinct as events of yesterday.　She
played a dirge, and the rich harmony of the
voice sank to a low, sad wail.　It changed to
a song of thanksgiving of Jewish maidens
after a victory.　The heart of the listener
bounded within him, beat quickly as the versa-

tile performer—the mistress of his thoughts
for the time being, poured forth songs of the
affections, breathing love never-dying, eternal.
" Music ! (writes a well-known authoress) that
is indeed an art.   The others can scarcely be
called so ; they have their types in nature—
they strive to imitate, or at least to glorify her.
Their aim is to idealise the human form and
human things—to ennoble the theatre on
which man acts ; it is a worthy aim, as is every
one which looks beyond the mere satisfaction of
material wants. But the marble god, the painted
virgin, are like ourselves—they walk with us
hand in hand.   Poetry, too, (the natural speech
of unsophisticated man) but gives us back our
own thoughts in our own language.   But
music, on the contrary, does not beautify this
world, its phenomena, but over arches it with
a second, in which we float like bodiless
cherubs with wings beneath a lovely confiding
face.   And this it effects through sounds
which are grounded upon numbers, by numbers represented, and from a combination of

wood and metal mysteriously, magically lured forth. According to careful, thoughtful, regular calculations, music will discover a new world above this earth as Columbus did upon it—a world full of primitive strength and splendour, a world in which each may seek his *eldorado :* and, indeed, a paradise, where, without having wisdom or penetration, and without understanding its laws, every one may enter who has a soul. Children, savages, grey beards, with minds too undeveloped or too blunted to enjoy the beauties of the chisel or the pencil, share the charms of music, and the lullaby and funeral hymn attend our first and last steps through life."

How long she had been singing or playing, Ernest could not tell. He took no note of time. He had lived whole ages in the past and future since Miss Fairweather had sat down and played the first note. He had tossed alternately on the billows of memory and imagination; old familiar faces had risen up to welcome him, the glory had returned to the grass, the freshness to the flower—he had lived over again his past life, and dashed boldly into the future—he had won fame with pencil and pen, and had stood in the Vatican and paid homage to Michael, and returned and poured out his love at the feet of a woman. In Miss Fairweather he had found the sympathising nature he had pined for so long, and she, this intelligent beautiful being might become his wife. Rapture!—a woman like this to cheer the lonely fireside—such eyes as those to grow brighter at thy approach—that fair soft hand to touch thy fevered brow—that voice to breathe its music in thine ear. Can all this beauty, this intellect, this poetry of existence be his. Will she count the moments of his absence, and get up and listen, and look forth, and murmur—" Oh, that my husband were come." Hark she is playing on the piano, he will steal up gently that he may hear his favorite air and take her by surprise. She has stopped—the ear of affection is too quick, she has heard your footstep—she rushes to meet and welcome you, her husband. Oh! happy Benedict, clasp your young wife to your bosom, take long, long kisses from those lips, turn those braids into curls. The music ceased, and Ernest returned from dream-land to the society of his mother and two young ladies, mentally determining that he would have a picture of Miss Fairweather. *Rum* creatures are young men. Disguise themselves as they will, yielding to the prejudices of the world and walking about in dress-coats, boots of patent leather, and starched collars, their hearts will nevertheless continue to beat and flutter. Certainly the great French Statesman was right — " Language was given us to conceal our thoughts." No one could have guessed from Ernest's common-place nothings as he saw the young ladies home that he had just been indulging in such romantic dreams.

He was, if anything, more silent than usual during the *tête-à-tête* with Miss Fairweather after leaving Miss Lawrence at home, and we have no doubt the former young lady thought him very stupid to lose so fair an opportunity, and gave him no credit for being in a transition state, too much in love for flirting, and not quite enough in love to speak out. After his return home, he said jocularly to his mother, " Suppose I propose to Miss Fairweather provided she is an heiress." His mother was so accustomed to his absurdities and to his being ever in love with some girl or other, that she never gave the question a thought, but kissed her son and bade him good night, leaving Ernest in a brown study, staring intently into the expiring embers ; for though it was summer, the day had been chilly enough for fire. At last starting up suddenly, he sat down at the table and began to write (like one who has made up his mind,) the following letter.

" MY DEAR MISS FAIRWEATHER,"

Our brief, and to me, agreeable acquaintance is soon to be discontinued by your return to Bonnar. Will you not think me too severely infringing the laws of etiquette, in thus seizing

an opportunity of thanking you before you depart, for the favour and benefit your society has
conferred upon me. In a letter we can often
explain ourselves more satisfactorily than by a
verbal communication. For this reason, and
because our personal interviews are not so
frequent as I at least could desire, I venture to
hope that you will excuse me for what I fear,
Miss Becky Blab would consider, an infraction
of strict conventional propriety. I will not
trespass further on your good nature, except to
say what gratification it would give me to receive
a reply to these lines should you think them
deserving of one. In either case I must beg
you to concede me the privilege of subscribing
myself your sincere friend and well-wisher,

ERNEST BASIL."

P.S. How rude and unaimiable you must
have thought me the other evening at the concert. All that I can say in extenuation is, that
I am so often and continually obliged to wear
a masque and pursue a line of conduct utterly

foreign to my real character, that my disposition and temper have suffered materially. In one point of view I can hardly regret the untoward circumstance, since it gave me an opportunity of an insight into the frankness and generosity of your nature.—E. B.

CHAPTER V.

MR. PENNYWISE CLOSE, THE GOOD YOUNG MAN—
HIS VICTIM.

WILL it be a glorious state of things when the
onward advance of civilization and progress
shall have halted and bivouacked at that station where the enemies, vice and folly, have been
completely routed and put *hors de combat.*
When there shall be no need of warnings and
examples for the rising generation, because
everybody will be himself an example to himself and everybody else. When there shall be
no occasion to lecture or punish a world so
wise, so gentle, and so good, that every individual will be minding his own business and pro-
ceeding incontinently to the discharge of his
own duty ; when people will know nothing but
what they ought to know, and do nothing but

what they ought to do; when the rich will be emulous of changing places with the poor, and the poor so contented and happy, such true philosophers, that they will not hear of it on any account; or when there will be no distinctions of rich and poor, but an universal equality of worldly as well as intellectual wealth, and beauty and knowledge; everyone will have the same number of acres, and exactly the same balance at his banker's, when the very memory of such words as bribery and corruption, scandal, avarice, pride, pestilence, famine, war, &c., shall be utterly forgotten, and the vices of play, betting and horse-racing, drinking, smoking, &c, will be as interesting monuments of a barbarian age as the relics of the ancient Britons.

Hail ye unborn ages, when the memory of a fast young man shall be handed down by tradition and we shall have infinitely more doubts of the existence of a " *downy cove*" than of the megatherium or the mastodon; when a latch key dug up from the ruins of ancient

London shall excite the speculation of the curious and the learned among posterity as the Ninevah remains are now doing. When among other changes which have taken place, the term governor shall no longer be applied to our masculine parent, and the popular enquiry " how's your mother; does she know you're out," otherwise rendered—" is your maternal relative aware of your absence from the domiciliary residence," shall have sunk into well-merited oblivion. When club-houses shall have disappeared and cab-drivers shall really make use of that respectable phraseology which by a fiction of the guide books they are believed by foreigners to use.

Nothing would seem a more glorious object for the ambition of the rising generation to aim at than the title of *a steady or a good young man*, and we believe the terms to be synonimous. Mr. Pennywise Close, already mentioned in these pages, is never defined in any other way. He is never spoken of as a rich, or a poor, or a talented, or a fast, (oh no, not he indeed) or

as anything else but *a good young man, a
steady young man.* But this, like the aphorism,
that people are no better than they should be,
has a signification different from the simple
meaning it apparently implies. We have often
observed that when people have no peculiarity
of character whatever, no bias, nor inclination
in any direction in particular, no fondness or
taste, or addiction, either to good or evil, or to
any mortal thing more than another, when in
short, they so nearly resemble *automata* that it
may seem a libel on them to consider their existence as anything but one continued daily mistake, then we speak of them in a very summary
manner as good. It may be a prejudice, but we
incline to think that it requires some *positive*
abilities, and not the mere absence of qualities
to be *good*. Something like a heart, a mind,
a soul; some active recognition of the principles of right and wrong, while practically we
find the shortest way of arriving at the distinction of *a good young man* is to say nothing,
feel nothing, and in short to approach as near as

possible, *nonentity*. Surely then, every person of good taste would beg to repudiate a reputation got in such a negative manner. If, gentle reader, you were about to verify the transmigration of Indor in your own person, would you not rather be a ferocious than a harmless animal. I think any person of good taste would prefer being changed to a *carnivorous* rather than a *ruminating* quadruped. The good young man is the latter, his keeper shall stir him up with a long pole and no further description beyond the name is necessary; a good young man implieth that there are no depths, no shoals, hills or valleys, lights or shadows; no inequalities or peculiarities of temper, or organisation of any kind for the showman or exhibitor to seize upon, without even the honour of inspiring awe or timidity, but perfectly tame—not in the least dangerous.

Though this sort of negative goodness imposes seriously upon society, it is pretty evident, that a man who cannot lay claim to any positive *good* qualities, must possess some po-

sitively *bad,* if we could but penetrate beneath
the cloak of hypocrisy sufficiently to discover
them. Mr. Pennywise Close possessed this
sort of negative character. He was never
known to have gone through the far from innocent process called "sowing wild oats." He
had never been dissipated like other young
men; no one had ever remembered to have
seen or heard that he had been intoxicated,
he neither drank, nor smoked, nor betted, nor
played, nor frequented theatres; in short he
had none of those sins of *commission* so rife
among young men. Very much in Mr. Close's
favour all these negative traits of character,
and so a great many people, especially among
his own sect, the Free Church, thought and
said.—"Prudent mamas spoke of him before
their daughters, as an extremely eligible well-
to-do young man. Mrs. Grainger talked of
him as just a wonder for a young man, and
even Miss Scunnerweel, who had hardly a
good word for anybody, admits that he's dis-
creet compared wi' the lave, while many an old

lady points him out to a wild nephew as a pattern and a model."

Unfortunately, however, for Mr. Close to be considered good in that court, where men shall not preside, the accusing angel will not forget our sins of omission as well as commission, and the recording scribe will note many benevolent and charitable actions, which *ought* to have been done. There were several other things which Mr. Close did not do besides the apparent omissions recorded. He had never refused a treat offered by a friend's liberality; and he had never been known to give one himself. It was indeed on record that he had at various times asked friends to sup with him at taverns. Yet these instances of seeming liberality must be added to the negative list, as on such occasions it has invariably happened that Mr. Close has forgotten his purse, and his friends have settled the bill, whether, owing to forgetfulness of such a trifling matter, Mr. Close has never got rid of the obligation. He has likewise asked friends at various times to ride with him in his one horse killer (brougham), but like those who went swimming with the dark lady, similar favours are not in request, as the guest in such instances Mr. Close has *permitted* to defray the tolls. In the matter of charity Mr. Close is decidedly *negative*, never has he suffered himself to be imposed upon by those well got up counterfeits of misery which prowl in the public streets, indeed where a common observer would have fancied a real object of distress, never does this clear-sighted young man relax from the severity of his principles, asserting his stoicism by a cheerful smile or witty jest as he passes the mendicant.

With respect to religion Mr. Close practices the same beautiful and convenient system of negative virtue, and by an agreeable and comfortable compromise between belief and works, makes *seeming* do in place of *being*. Thus, he believes the theory that charity covereth a multitude of sins, that it is good to succour the helpless and oppressed, to visit the widow and orphans in their affliction, only *he doesn't do it.*

But he goes regularly to the Free Kirk every Sunday, and listens patiently to Mr. Muckle-whackit, who preaches literally a *thumping* sermon on faith and good works, who alternately holds one or the other respectively as the only means of being saved, there—Mr. Close stops naturally enough—since he finds that this weekly formula obtains him the credit of being religious at all the respectable families where he visits. He knows by experience what punctual attendance at church, will do for a young man in the eyes of his own congregation, at least, lulling to sleep, suspicions of grievious deficiencies in practical morality. Every Sabbath then Mr. Close may be observed, with carefully smoothed hair, looking sleek and religious, as he joins in the psalm, and thereby giving the lie to any aspersions of his enemies during the week. Who would believe anything against *such a religious young man*, so promising a mark for the admiration of the minister and congregation, reflecting credit on themselves and the institution to which they belong, which could thus train to such hot-house perfection, so pious a plant.

In politics Mr. Close is most negative, or, to use a paradox, negative in the most positive degree. He is conservative. Without the ambition or the energy to struggle for more learning, wealth, or fame, than he finds himself in possession of, he of course objects to any change which would give the honest and industrious poor a better chance, and by equalising wealth and happiness, rob him of any of his comforts and luxuries. What can the people want now. Can the state of society be better than that which I find ready made to my hand says this selfish philosopher with about the same perception of the conditions and wants of humanity as the snail in its shell. In this age of progress, civilisation, enlightenment, and morality, to talk of the condition of the labouring classes. Phsaw! I should like ten thousand a year instead of six hundred. There is some ingenuity in Mr. Close's philosophy. It simplifies very much all those complicated questions of political and social economy, to look at them through the medium of number one, to keep our own particular circumstances, wants and wishes ever in the foreground. As the skeleton presided at Egyptian feasts so let the shadow of our own individuality regulate all our sympathies and we shall at once solve difficulties which would keep other men groping in the dark, life-long. This was Mr. Close's method. He would lay down a scale of duties quite at variance with that propounded by Cicero, who declares our first duty is to God, our second to our country, and the third to our parents, leaving our poor unfortunate selves last of all, distanced, nowhere. Mr. Penny-wise Close makes it his first duty to take care of *himself*, his second duty to take care of *him-self*, his third duty to take care of *himself*. His days pass by in the pleasant routine of eating, drinking, and sleeping, minding the main chance, setting the utmost value on his money, enjoying himself with his dogs, and horses, and generally surrounding himself with all the luxuries and comforts which his snug little income will afford. As long as Mr. Pennywise Close can do these things, he is not likely to change his views, social, political, or religious, or that he will ever grow metaphysical and trouble himself with awkward queries like Hamlet's. " What should such fellows as I do crawling between heaven and earth ?"

Mr. Close has descended from a race of skinflints, his father was a skinflint, and *his* father before him. His parent had indeed christened his son Pennywise, from a laudable desire to stamp for ever on his mind the importance of the one thing needful in his opinion—money. There was likewise a baronetcy in the family to which, it seemed very probable that this estimable young man would succeed, and this may have something to do with the good odour, which he preserved in society in spite of some ugly scandals with which his name had been associated. One of them was as follows :—About a year previous when Ernest first came to reside in Y——, the sudden disappearance of a young and beautiful female called Ellen Douglas, had caused much gossip in the community. Ellen was one of a class whose lot in a provincial town is peculiarly hard. She was beautiful and had been educated for a superior station to that which she occupied, a milliner's apprentice. We wonder if society feels no compunction for the influence it exerts over these poor girls' destiny, and for the numbers which her harsh unjust treatment assists to destroy. Ellen was tall beautiful and young; but she had none of the usual license granted to *young ladies*. *They* might dress themselves in new bonnets and new shawls every day, be as idle, as affected as they pleased. *They* might walk with officers along the principal street of Y——, or be flirted with and talked nonsense to by the hour, and scandal would not dare to assail them, because they were *young ladies*, rich and of course subject to another law of morality than the poor dressmaker. But if Ellen's tall form were seen in

Grafton Street, Miss Scunnerweel and Miss Becky Blab and a host of others, were immediately down on "*that creature's depravity*, never off the streets glintin' at aw the young men," and if she appeared in a new bonnet " whatever a bizness had the like of sic hizzies, aping their betters in dress." Miserably unjust society, as if youth and beauty in every station of life were not intended to enjoy and inspire happiness.

In an evil hour Ellen Douglas had become acquainted with Mr. Pennywise Close. Had she known his real character, she would have loathed and detested him, but Mr. Close was an accomplished hypocrite. Ellen Douglas had no one to love or cling to. Ernest had noticed in the course of his rambles at the window of a cottage in the suburbs of Y—— a fair, young, and pale face, whose beauty was heightened by the look of melancholy which sat on the features. More than once he had met Mr. Close in the neighbourhood. Once he had seen him enter the house, from the window of which the face, lightened up

with an unusual expression of joy, had just
disappeared. Shortly afterwards the beautiful
face was seen no more at the window, and then
a report circulated that Ellen Douglas had left
Y——. Who places credit in half one hears?
—who was to know how much truth or falsehood there was in the various rumours. Some
said Ellen had been turned out of the house
in a condition to move the stoniest heart to
pity, and that her seducer had abandoned her
at a time when common humanity should have
pleaded in her favour.   It was even said that
by the law of Scotland Close was legally married to his victim, but that he had taken steps
to get rid of the witnesses who could have
proved it.   Be this as it may, Ellen Douglas
had never appealed to the law, and people are
prone to believe the worst.   She was gone,
and in a short time forgotten.   If the report
had ever reached those with whom it could
have injured Mr. Close, his brazen effrontery
had enabled him to fight through all suspicion,
for it is astonishing how difficult it is to know

the exact truth of occurrences happening apparently within our sphere of observation. Then Mr. Close found the value of his reputation as a good religious young man. His admirers were indignant at the attempt to slander the character of so regular an attendant at kirk. "If it had been ony wild graceless ne'er-do-weel, we might hae believed it, but to couple Mr. Close's name with that of a shameless hizzie like yon Ellen Douglas." Thus by degrees, as the excitement blew over, and Mr. Close still continued to sit and sing hymns under Mr. Mucklewhackit, his fame as a good young man was established on a more sure basis than ever, and some pitied him as in some degree a martyr.

CHAPTER VI.

ERNEST hardly knew whether to join Miss
Fairweather and Miss Lawrence when he met
them on the day following that on which his
note had been sent. After the thing was
done, he felt misgivings about the propriety of
sending it. He feared that Miss Fairweather
might, and yet he hardly thought she *would*,
resent it as a liberty. What if it had fallen
into the hands of the dragon who guarded the
Hesperian fruit, — Mrs. Grainger, who, with
the peculiar delicacy of her system for bringing up young ladies to be frank and honest,
opened all Miss Fairweather's letters. But
recollecting the adage—" Faint heart, &c.,"
and setting gossip at defiance, he joined the

young ladies in Grafton Street. His conversation was not indeed singularly brilliant, for his doubts as to the posture of affairs, and his anxiety to guess from Miss Fairweather's looks whether she had received his note, gave a good deal of constraint to his address. As for Miss Fairweather, it was impossible to guess by her manner or conversation whether she had seen the note, and Miss Flaccid's approach proved the signal for Ernest to bid adieu after having obtained Miss Fairweather's acceptance of Bryant's poems as a souvenir of their acquaintance. As soon as he went home he sent her the book, accompanied by a short note. That evening and all next day passed without bringing any reply, much to Ernest's astonishment and mortification.

As he was returning home about nine in the evening, he came suddenly upon Miss Fairweather and Miss Lawrence coming from the Flaccids', and naturally offered his escort to see them home. Ernest could not help noticing, not at all to the increase of his good

nature and powers of rendering himself agreeable, that there was a sort of constraint in Miss
Fairweather's manner towards him, which appeared half frightened, and half distant.   On
their way they encountered no less a personage
than Mrs. Grainger; and Miss Fairweather
said, in a whisper quite audible to Ernest—

"Oh, she will think I met him by appoint-
ment at the Flaccids'."

Mrs. Grainger looked particularly grim at
Ernest as she spoke to the young ladies, and
then continued on her way in the opposite direction.   No introduction took place as, under
the circumstances should have been the case,
and Ernest was not a little annoyed at the want
of good manners.   A pleasant reward this,
he thought, as he walked beside Miss Fairweather without opening his lips, for, behaving
with common politeness, a mere stranger
could hardly have done less than I have done.
Yet the young lady who but the other evening
at my mother's house captivated me by the
frankness of her manners, now freezes me with

her coldness, and my peace of mind is further disturbed, not by the blood-boltered Banquo smiling, but by the Free Church lady scowling on me. My good Ernest Basil, you are not the first, nor will you be the last doomed to disappointment, if he expects to take young ladies up where he left them. It is certainly very unpleasant to have to speak the honeyed language of conventional politeness, when we are absolutely burning with a desire to put a straightforward question and receive a straightforward answer. Ernest could have ground his teeth with rage as he mechanically shaped the words of formal leave-taking. " She might at least have gone through the ceremony of asking me in," he said, as he walked home pondering on and perplexing himself as to the cause of mystery, and wondering whether he would put it in his own power to have a third misunderstanding with Miss Fairweather. He arrived at home cursing the caprice of young ladies, and wondering whether there was such a thing as a warm heart in Scotland.

On going into the parlour where his mother and Miss Saunders were playing at chess, his quick eye discovered at once a letter lying on the table, and directed to himself in a female hand.

"Look," said Miss Saunders. "what I have for you; a *billet doux*, I am sure."

Ernest took it up, and all the quizzing in the world would not have detracted from the pleasure he felt in the contents of that letter.

" Miss Fairweather thanked him in the most cordial terms for his little souvenir, and was exceedingly gratified with his first note, though very much astonished at receiving it, for she had no idea that their acquaintance, though a source of the greatest possible enjoyment to *her*, could have afforded *him* the slightest pleasure or amusement."

If Ernest did not go through the expressive pantomime of kissing this note, he might have done so, so great was the relief which it afforded after his previous despondence. He sat down immediately to write an answer.

The ice of epistolatory correspondence once broken, hardly a day passed for some months without Mr. Basil and Miss Fairweather mutually sending and receiving a letter. Very nice sensible letters they were too, for no absolute avowal of love had yet taken place, (although they were certainly very complimentary to one another) and as long as a gentleman and lady are only *friends*, they may write as well as talk sense. A couple of extracts from letters which passed between Ernest and a confidential friend in Edinburgh about this time may likewise serve to throw some light upon the state of matters between Miss Fairweather and her admirer.

Frank Berton to Ernest Basil.

" Going it as usual, my dear Ernest, I find; endeavouring to break hearts by the score. I like your idea of making a list of all your lady friends, with the peculiar qualities and accomplishments of each attached to her name, so that by massing the whole you may form that fearful and indescribable thing — *a perfect woman.* **Why** it would beat Frankenstein's monster. Rather cool in you to write, though, that you are in love with several—*several*, indeed, well done, modest young man, would not one at a time content you? And yet I think I understand you. You mean that in lieu of finding in one woman all those qualities necessary to enchant and to enslave such a cormorant as yourself, you make up as you best can your ideal from several, and draw from each the particular consolation which her society is able to afford. Thus you enjoy a laugh with one, a song from another, a dance with a third, and so on; one charms by her beauty, another by her wit, another by her good nature; one you could love for her refined tastes and accomplishments, another for her rich voice, or beautiful figure, or a pair of black eyes, or—or—*because you couldn't help it.* And you, fastidious happy dog, have the face to complain of your lot. You are the strangest compound of philosophy, love, business, and pleasure, reason and nonsense, conceit and

humility, I ever *met in* with, as the Scotch say.
However, I must give you credit for hinting at
some new acquaintance you have made lately
in some terms of sincerity. I should be
amazed if my prophecy were fulfilled, and you
should meet in Y—— the nymph destined to
the great achievement of fixing the affections
of that inconstant rover, Ernest Basil. You
must tell me something about this fair lady
who seems likely to work this miracle, and
render harmless the gallant gay Lothario hitherto roaming round the world like a certain
gentleman who shall be nameless, and not even
confining, himself to one hemisphere, in his
unceasing business of heart-fracturing. It will
be retributive justice to smart a little in your
turn. But if you *are serious,* all I can say in
my present state of ignorance is—' Look before you leap.' "

Ernest Basil to Frank Berton.

With regard to a certain young lady whom
I mentioned in my last, and whose acquaintance is becoming of such daily increasing in-

terest to me, that not even to such an intimate
friend as you are, do I feel authorised at present in mentioning her name; but simply as a
young lady I may write much which I would
not otherwise reveal. She is then the most
superior girl I have yet met in Y——, indeed,
as far as I can judge, the most superior I have
ever met. How much above the cold conventional creature of etiquette you will at once
guess, when I tell you that we correspond together like rational beings, and that our letters
are not about love as yet. I can't help feeling
that there are strong links of sympathy between us. I write to her and pour out the
most poetic feelings of my soul, and she gives
evidence both in her letters and conversation
that she understands me thoroughly. Whatever may be the result of this friendship (I
will not call it acquaintance), is it not a boon
to one situated as I am in Y——, to possess
such sympathy, you can well understand dear
Berton, that my esteem and admiration for
such a one, prompt me to be so very particular

even to the verge of unnecessary mystery
about a confidence of this nature conveyed
in a letter. You can understand and appre-.
ciate my motives, and should you by any
chance discover her name before I am at liberty to reveal it, I know it would be superfluous to ask you to consider what I have
told you in the light of a *solemn confidence*. Is it not delightful Berton to find
such a friend in woman, a young lady with
whom you can soar beyond trivialities and
common-place. Who can penetrate beneath the starch and varnish with which society
compels both men and women to conceal their
real characters. Such in our brief acquaintance
of three months I have found this young lady
to be, and yet it is only by letter I may say,
that we are enabled to communicate. She
lives with very strict people who seem to be
afraid of her looking at a young man. She is
only twenty, how young to be so accomplished,
to possess such just and refined feelings. She
has been partially educated in Germany, and is

a French and German scholar.   It is not the proper term to call her a perfect musician.   If you were to hear her play and sing she would bewitch you as she did me; and now I come to her personal appearance; you ask me if she is handsome? That she is, and yet I will not deny that, tried by the strict rules of art, Miss Lawrence, another lady-friend, is even more beautiful than the fair unknown.   No description can succeed in conjuring up before you her face and figure as I recall them at this moment, yet I will try.   In height she somewhat exceeds the middle size, her figure is symmetrical, and she moves and stands with perfect dignity and grace: but that face, the mingled effect of regularity of features and intellectual expression, the nose between straight and aquiline, the mouth neither large nor small, the eyes large and deep blue, the eyebrow clearly defined, the forehead majestic, and the rich clustering brown hair waving over it, and descending in long curls almost to the waist, her complexion, a pure red and white,

not those fierce blood-red roses that you often
see in this country, but the cheek just deep-
ened a little in colour, like an American beauty.
Imagine the witchery of expression joined to
all those traits of beauty, and you may form
some faint idea of Constance Fairweather—yet,
really it is not for her personal beauty I admire her. I believe I have, indeed I know I
have seen in New York handsomer women,
and I certainly thought Miss Lawrence handsomer at first; but Miss Fairweather has
awakened in my heart more serious feelings
than I knew I possessed. I confess when I
first made her acquaintance, I saw in her only
another young lady added to my list. I pursued the acquaintance for some time with no
other idea than that of banishing *ennui* by
talking nonsense and flirting as I perhaps have
done too often before; but with Miss Fairweather I find myself substituting unconsciously earnest conversation for idle badinage. The acquaintance vanished and friend-

ship began. A few more weeks or months may decide this critical point whether we are to forget one another, or whether she is to be to me the ministering angel for which my spirit pines unceasingly. My heart thrills at the thought, will this fair and gentle being ever come to be associated with all my thoughts, hopes, feelings, fill up the void in my heart ; already my memory wanders back less frequently to past scenes, friends, and affections. Yet, where is my imagination wandering to, You will think me in love already and that I am not, on the verge I may be, but no man is in love when he can ask,—do I love or not? *Love* knows no doubts, no fears ; it neither reasons nor hesitates, nor asks the advice of friends. It is self-judging, decided, imperious. I must break off, I hear her voice, and Miss Lawrence's in the parlour—

" — Oh, Berton, I have just time to add this line to tell you I have just obtained her promise to sit for her picture. What a picture I

will paint of her. Shall it be in character—
as a queen—a Juno—a Judith—a Miranda—
will it not be better to paint her exactly as she
is, to copy those features carefully, to transfer
her living, breathing image to the canvass. I
think so. What say you. Farewell.

ERNEST BASIL.

CHAPTER VII.

SEVERAL sittings had already taken place, and the picture certainly ought to have been further advanced than it was, and would have been probably, had Ernest been painting a less handsome young lady. But it really is none of our business, if it went on fast enough to please the parties concerned. We purpose in this chapter to record a *tête-à-tête* between the artist and his sitter, Miss Lawrence not being present as she was in general.

Miss Fairweather was indulging in one of those interesting fits of silence which formed a contrast to her usual lively manner, and seemed to find a pleasure in listening to Ernest, who was gradually talking more and painting less.

" No, Miss Fairweather, it is difficult to get

the credit of seeing beauty *as an artist.* I
pass a girl in humble life, without fashion or
dress or elegance to set her off to advantage.
But nature has chiselled her features in a
classic mould, and given her a graceful figure
and elastic step. I see all this at a glance,
and cannot help exclaiming to my unsympa-
thising companion for the time being, Flaccid,
or any one else—' How beautiful.' He looks
and sees only a poor girl beneath that sphere
where he looks for beauty, gives me an incredulous stare to see if I am joking, bursts into
a stupid laugh and says—' Oh, you think
everybody beautiful.' And so everybody *is*
beautiful, and how much beauty blooms un-
heeded by man, who goes blundering through
the world minding the main chance, admiring,
according to modern conventional rules, blind
as a bat where beauty is concerned. The
poet and the artist, and all who possess in any
degree what is called the creative power, know
and feel that the world is full of beauty. They
are said by the multitude to invent, when they

only seize upon a few out of the immeasureable glories of existence, and put them before the admiring gaze of their fellow men. Artists, poets, philosophers, authors, musicians, sculptors, &c., *invent*, in the original meaning of the world, they discover. The artist who worships the Greek ideal, does not necessarily ignore beauty existing in types essentially different. But the triumphs of the Greek school seem to be founded on the truest and most profound principles of beauty, if we may judge by the universal sympathy they have excited in creative minds in all ages. If we had never seen them, we should desire to see the works which could have so inspired Byron, where, speaking of the Apollo, he says—

> " But in his delicate form—a dream of love
> Shaped by some solitary nymph, whose breast
> Long'd for a deathless lover from above,
> And madden'd in that vision—are exprest
> All that ideal beauty ever bless'd
> The mind with in its most unearthly mood
> When each conception was a heavenly guest—
> A ray of immortality—and stood
> Starlike, around, until they gather'd to a god."

" One would, indeed," said Miss Fairweather. " Tell me where those beautiful lines are, that I may read them when I go home."

" I will show them to you, Miss Fairweather," said Ernest, taking up a small pocket edition of Byron, and turning to the fourth canto of Childe Harold. " There is a religion in art," he continued, " a feeling which gains on the heart of the true and devout worshipper. Look at yonder bust of Clytæ, Miss Fairweather. How often have I drawn it and hung upon its surpassing loveliness, till it began to exercise a sort of spell over me while contemplating the tempered pride conveyed in that short curling lip, and the soul which looks out at the full almond-shaped eyes, drooping at the outer extremities, and the serene majesty of that over arching intellectual brow, and as I gazed I fancied I could sympathise with Pygmalion, in the craze which stole over me, wondering whether such a living form existed, or might be found perchance on earth."

" Do you know who I think it like ?" said Miss Fairweather. " Miss Lawrence. She has the same grand classic outline, the same drooping eye, and curling lip."

" There is indeed a resemblance," said Ernest, " I have often thought so. It struck me very much when I first saw Miss Lawrence."

" What a pity," said Miss Fairweather, " that art should not be better understood, and better reward its votaries."

" We must not," said Ernest, " fall into the common error of measuring an artist's happiness, as we would a stockbroker's, by his wealth. Why should they be pitied for not growing rich. There is something enviable in carrying for ever with us that exquisite sense of beauty which creates a paradise for the artist and the poet out of the most homely scenes. They feel like Wordsworth when he wrote that beautiful sonnet beginning—

> The world is too much with us ;
> Getting and spending we lay waste our powers.

To them even with advancing years the world does not put off all the beauty and freshness it wore in youth, for they do not view its glories merely in glimpses out of a host of cares, and disappointments, and grasping avarice. They have not bartered their birthright for the false glitter of worldly honours, for the dross which delights the short-sighted sage called the man of the world. Is it no privilege to reflect in the decline of life that time has not been one continued loss, in idly squandering inherited wealth, and grasping at inordinate riches, in speculations of low cunning, or permitting talents to lie dormant. Such are the men whom the insolent worldling, the office-seeker, the bauble-hunter, the trafficker in human blood, the base sinecurist, dare to call idle dreamers, and why, because they have not smothered and over-laid every trace of divinity within in their hearts—because, instead of sacrificing at the shrine of mammon and *dishonour*, they have avoided the selfish contaminating strife, and preferred to dwell with nature, to be ' the pale and silent worshipper in woods,' rather than the degraded beings of a spurious civilisation. It was not idly dream-

ing to read the book of nature, to gaze upon
'·the stars which are the poetry of heaven,' and
feel a vitality which the worldling can never
know."

The artist had risen unconsciously from his
seat while thus speaking, or rather thinking
aloud, and stood partially leaning against the
wall with the palette in his hand in an attitude
which displayed his tall figure to great advantage. Miss Fairweather thought he had never
seemed so handsome as when, with sparkling
eye, he continued to pour out his thoughts with
such vehemence and fluency.

" You speak well in defence of your art,
Mr. Basil."

" I had need to do so," was his reply,
dropping at once into his usual half-jocular
tone of voice. " Some people have such odd
ideas of a painter. He is synonimous in their
eyes with all that is eccentric and *outré*. Miss
Flaccid thinks me very odd, and Miss Greenshields had the impudence to say the other day
to my very face, she wondered how artists ever

expected to be married. It must be so stupid, she said, to have a husband sitting at his easel all day and never opening his lips."

" I agree with her there, I think it would be very stupid."

" Yes, but are we poor artists to expect no sympathy, are our wives to take no interest in our pursuits? I have known artists with beautiful wives who went to Italy with them and accompanied them in their sketching tours and never wearied in their husbands' company. I have known officers' ladies in Canada who used to go out with their husbands on the coldest days in winter, and even learnt to walk on snow shoes and skate; and seemed never to weary of the society of the man they loved. How much better this than a poor delicate wife who can only be company for her husband in doors and expects him to be tied to her apron strings. Besides you have no idea how happy and merry painters can be; they do not sit silent all the time they are at work, as you have had an opportunity of observing."

" No, it is only when you get very much absorbed, indeed, that you don't talk ; yet for the
last half-hour you have not born out your
theory or else these touches, so few and far between, must have some magical power in producing the effect."

" Indeed, Miss Fairweather, it would become
you rather to be my apologist than my accuser,
seeing that you are the enchantress who has
laid a spell upon me. Can I help it if in painting you my hand has lost its cunning, or if I
feel disposed to throw aside my brushes in despair, when I compare my efforts and the
original."

" Mr. Basil, I don't like being laughed at."

" In sad sober earnest, I shall never be able
to get this mouth to please me. Look for
yourself, if you are incredulous." Somewhat
mollified by the serious tone in which this was
said, Miss Fairweather rose and approached
the picture. Side by side stood the artist and
his lovely sitter, and a very pretty group the
two made, Ernest with his black hair and mous-

tache, his pale almost sallow features brightened up with conscious pleasure. Constance veiling her beautiful blue eyes in a downcast look, as if bent on criticising the picture, but in reality listening attentively to every word which fell from her companion, who was first changing from the heroic into a complimentary vein, or rather couching real sincerity under a tone of badinage.

" It will be like, I think," said he, " unfinished and imperfect as it now looks, when I have put into it a little more of the beauty of the original."

" How can you, Mr. Basil—running on in that way, just as if I swallowed it all like every silly girl to whom you repeat the same nonsense."

" How is it Miss Fairweather that I am fated to be misunderstood when I am most in earnest? But.

> T'was ever thus from childhood's hour
> I've seen my fondest hopes decay.

No sooner do I attempt to express the real

feelings of my heart than I am accused of idly complimenting."

Miss Fairweather did not interrupt, as if willing to see how far the conceit would carry him and how much of earnest there was in his words.

" I have, indeed, great cause to say," continued Ernest—

> Oh that the desert were my dwelling place,
> With one fair spirit for my minister,
> That I might all forget the human race,
> And hating no one love but only her.

" Young ladies in general, I am sorry to say, have much to answer for. How often have we desired to cultivate their acquaintance, to soar with them beyond the dull region of common place nothings, to talk with them on metaphysics, or weep over the sorrows of that extremely doubtful martyr of modern history, Uncle Tom, to wander with them into the realms of Fairy Land, into green fields, by the sides of rivers and highland hills, or by the ocean wave ; we would have studied conchology together by picking up shells on the shore, or geology by chipping rocks with little hammers ; botany by picking wild flowers ; or we would have sketched with them the streams flowing pleasantly up-hill, and smoke, despising the natural laws by going against the wind. Alas ! that such delightful visions could not be realized ; alas, that a few conventional ideas, and crozier and berlin wool should have come between us and happiness. Alas ! that these hateful occupations under the title of *work* should be esteemed young ladies missions, should engross their hands and their eyes, and that the heart yearning for sympathy should be maddened by monotonous sounds which convey no meaning to any sane masculine mind, such as *one*, *two*, pearl *three*. Beyond the schottische and polka we have sought communion in vain, and when they sang they tantalised us with visions, which mamas and maiden aunts would never permit to be fulfilled ; such as dancing over the highlands together."

" Havn't you done talking nonsense yet,

Mr. Basil, because you can talk so sensibly when you choose?"

" Go on by all means, bruise a broken reed, Miss Fairweather; affect to doubt my vehement protestations, make my solemn complaints food for mirth."

" But dear me, I am forgetting how the time goes. Mrs. Grainger will give me such a scolding."

" And when will you give me another · sitting."

" Really, it is impossible for me to say, it all depends on Mrs. Grainger. She thinks it is only a slight sketch."

" Mrs. Grainger appears to be my rock-a-head. If she would only call on my mother as I expected, and as in common propriety she ought, I might then call at your house and not trust altogether to the uncertainty of these sittings for seeing you. I should like so much to call."

" Would you," said Miss Fairweather, catching eagerly at the words, " I feel sure—I am persuaded—I mean—I think Mrs. Grainger would be very happy to see you."

" If you think I might venture, I certainly will, and yet I tremble at the idea of facing that pillar of Free Church orthodoxy in her own castle."

" Oh, for goodness sake don't differ with her on religious topics. If you say anything against the Free Church she will hate you."

" Never fear, on my head be it, if 1 offend her Calvinistic scruples."

" And—and did you get my last letter ?"

" Yes, and I have got two sheets nearly covered in reply, there they lie on my desk. I was busy writing when you came."

" Give them to me just as they are," said Miss Fairweather with a voice and look there was no resisting ; so the letter was folded and secreted in Miss Fairweather's reticule before Mrs. Basil, who had left the room for an instant, could witness the manœuvre. Yet though, she lost this, she might have noticed Ernest accompanying Miss Fairweather to the outer door, where he lingered speaking to her till she was half way down stairs and he had caught the last glimpse of her upturned smiling countenance which haunted him during the rest of the day.

CHAPTER VIII.

MRS. GRAINGER was a very fair specimen of
a bigotted Free Church lady—an automaton
wound up to attend so many religious meetings,
subscribe to so many charities, distribute so
many tracts, listen to so many sermons, read
so many chapters in the Bible, and spend so
much of each day in gossiping about her
neighbours. She laboured with all the little
zealous secular spirit of a partisan at an elec-
tion, in the cause of religion, (as she understood it) that is, to advance the interest of her
sect and her sect alone. Beyond its narrow
limits she sees neither Christianity nor civilisation, nor progress, nor brotherly love. Just
in proportion as she is sincere and zealous in
behalf of her own religious fraternity, is she

narrow, bigotted, and unjust, and prejudiced against all other denominations of her fellow Christians. She would trample without hesitation on every scheme of church government but her own, destroy all liberty of conscience, and none should be allowed to do good unless in her own petty way.

The Free Church lady entertains a holy horror of the Pope. Why, she cannot exactly tell, and we can only account for it as that instinctive antipathy with which all true followers of Calvin regard the successor of St. Peter. She thinks every church bad but her own, and the only shades of evil are in proportion as they recede from or approach to the *teaching* of " *that dear man,*" the Rev. Saunders Mucklewhackit, delivered with many violent contortions of body, and tremendous blows on the innocent pulpit cushion. At her house may be seen at all hours of the day, but especially at dinner time, a number of heavy-looking men in black, with white *choakers*, and remarkably good appetites. Were they less

indolent and clumsy, they might be mistaken for
unpolished waiters, but when they sit down to
table, they are discovered to be bright and shining luminaries of the Free Church, whose theo-
logical pursuits have so engrossed their time,
that the external cultivation of the manners
has not yet begun. These men constitute the
living idols, the saints and demi-gods, cannon-
ized upon earth, idolized more than any image
by the most devout Roman Catholic, the subject of the " *hero worship*" which forms so great
a feature in Free Church religion, and were it
not that their sacred characters are proof
against vanity and self-glorification, it would
be perhaps necessary to instruct the precentor
to add to his other functions the enunciation
of the memorable words uttered by the slave to
the triumphing Roman general—" Remember
thou art a man."

Whoever saw the Free Church lady when
she was not in a desperate hurry going to or
returning from some religious meeting or
other? What between Free Church charitable

associations, Free Church school meetings, Free Church lectures, Free Church meetings of sympathy, and meetings of indignation, and tea meetings, and prayer meetings, and nondescript meetings for some important purpose, without which the world might forget to revolve, the time of the Free Church lady is as much occupied as that of the celebrated Mrs. Jellaby (whose name indeed she has got according to Flaccid) of Borryoboolagha. The conversation of the Free Church lady is exactly such a mixture of devoutness, seasoned with scandal, as her avocations would lead you to expect. If religion consists in always talking about sermons, praising this or " *that dear man*," and wondering what can make Mr. and Mrs. —— go to hear such a *dry* preacher, or how any one can be satisfied with any doctrine short of that comforting *skreed* of pulpit eloquence concocted and poured forth by the Rev. Saunders Mucklewhackit, or, indeed, how anybody can take an interest in anything out of the pale of the Free Church ;

then it must be confessed that Mrs. Grainger
is a most religious woman. She takes no interest in the news or topics of the day beyond
the immediate circle of her neighbours' affairs,
nor can she even bear to discuss the prospects
of Christianity at home or abroad, except in
so far as they are connected with the advancement of the Free Church, her darling hobby :
all is vanity and vexation of spirit, in which
" *the dear men*" have not a finger.

Mrs. Grainger is too practically pious to
have time for any abstract discussions on spiritual things, on faith, hope, or charity, for
there is to be a great indignation meeting
against the Pope, or the Grand Duke of Tus-
cany, or some foreign power, which, by the
impartial discharge of its own laws, has in
some mysterious way or other offended against
the *majesty* or the *humility* (?) of the Free
Church of Scotland. And away rushes our
good Free Church lady to listen to one of the
dear men on the platform thundering denun-
ciations against his fellow-men and fellow-

Christians to an admiring audience, and pandering with fulsome adulation to the pride, prejudice, bigotry, fanaticism, narrow sectarian spirit of this *Christian* audience forsooth. And this is the chief relaxation of this religious woman who professes to be superior to all the rational intellectual amusements around her, to look down with patronising pity upon her less bigotted brethren who are bringing up their families to be intelligent, accomplished, and *sincere*, who allow in moderation the harmless pleasures fitted to the season of youth.

The Free Church lady is not more given to scandal than people of prejudiced and uncultivated minds usually are. But when she is not actually in Church, or practically engaged in some active *piece of piety*, she possesses no large or liberal ideas, or refined tastes, or love of literature to occupy her mind to the exclusion of paltry gossip upon trivial things. It will invariably be found that people religious after her fashion make a fair and impartial division of their time between their devotional

and family duties, and making themselves acquainted with all the little items of scandal in
the neighbourhood. On such food her pious
mind unbends and refreshes itself after the
arduous duties of devotion.

No wonder if Ernest felt somewhat nervous
as he knocked at the door of Mrs. Grainger's
abode, and was ushered into the august presence of that lady. Mrs. Grainger, as far as
personal appearance went, was one of those
women whom it was difficult to describe from
the absence of any salient features about her.
It was difficult to say how old she was, one
would never think of guessing her age. She
looked as if she had never been younger, and
never intended to get older. Anywhere between forty and sixty would have done for her.
She wore three curls on each side of her head,
and one might have known Mrs. Grainger for
ten years, and yet been taken back if asked
to state at a word whether these curls were her
own or *false*—let us say fictitious as a more
becoming word in speaking of anything con-

nected with Mrs. Grainger. Somehow or other Mrs. Grainger, taken in the abstract, conveyed the idea of such a woman as might be manufactured to order at a toy maker's or furniture warehouse. At a first general view, she looked very much like one of those female figures carved out of wood which generally accompany Noah's Arks for children, and are intended either for the patriarch's wife, or the wife of some one or the other of his sons.

She received Ernest, looking a little more pleasantly than when he had met her the other evening, and desired him, in a strong provincial accent, to " come off the door and sit intill the fire," for the prevailing easterly winds made a fire grateful, although in midsummer. Having complied with the request in its modified interpretation, Ernest opened the campaign by apologising for the liberty he had taken in calling, but he came to see whether Miss Fairweather's engagements permitted her to favour him with another sitting for the *sketch* which he was taking of her. He fol-

lowed this up by some general remarks calculated to have a conciliating effect on Mrs.
Grainger, and at length, by dint of an hour's
occasional conversation, in which he had drawn
out that good lady enough to gratify her, and
amuse Miss Fairweather and Miss Lawrence,
who came in shortly after him, taking care not
to contradict her in any of her hobbies, the
Free Church lady evidently began to incline
a favorable ear to her visitor, and when he had
presented the charitable fund with half-a-crown,
looked upon him in the light of a brand which
might possibly be snatched from the burning.

" Deed then, Mr. Basil, it is gratifying to
observe that, though educate in a prelatical
church, you hae correct ideas on many points.
Gin ye would gang to Mr. Mucklewhackit's
lectures to young men, ye would receive jist a
power of guid."

" I shall take care not to miss them,
ma'am. I do not doubt I shall find Mr. Mucklewhackit very entertaining—that is, *instruc-
tive* I should have said. I am always fond of

listening to Scottish preachers, they always appear to be so much in earnest. They speak so energetically, and make the dust fly so from the pulpit cushion, that it is quite edifying to listen to them; not like Mr. Stickler or Mr. Formula and other clergymen of our church, who stand bolt upright in the pulpit as if they had swallowed a ram rod for breakfast, or feared to waken any of the congregation whom they have sent to sleep."

"Constance, do ye mind whether it'll be Wednesday or Thursday yon converted priest lectures on the abuses of nunneries. Will your friend Miss Lawrence be for ganging wi' us?"

"My dear Mrs. Grainger," said the last mentioned young lady, with something like a quizzical expression of countenance, "I do not think the most eloquent lecturer in the world could inspire me with greater scruples against the profession of a nun, than I possess at present. I have always thought it would be a great piece of injustice, not only to myself, but to all my friends, to seclude myself from the world. Constance, do you feel particularly desirous of taking the veil?" Constance laughed and blushed, and replied in the negative, while Mrs. Grainger, who was not blessed with quick perceptions of the ludicrous, looked grave and said nothing.

Ernest interrupted the silence—

" I hope," he said to Mrs. Grainger, " soon to be able to congratulate you on your son passing his examinations. He is *grinding* very hard, he told me, *cramming* as they would call it in England, or in the college in British America where I graduated."

" What," said Miss Fairweather, " are you a graduate of a college ?"

" I possess the privilege of writing bachelor of arts after my name."

" Oh, aye," said Mrs. Grainger, with a sort of contemptuously compassionate tone, " but these transatlantic colleges will no be vera particular."

In spite of Ernest's wish to overlook all

Mrs. Grainger's short comings in propriety, he could not help wincing at this last ill-bred remark, as he observed—

" At the college where I graduated—a British college with English and Scotch professors—the examinations for an A.B. degree were more difficult than they are here. And certainly Horace, Homer, and Euclid are as difficult in America as in Scotland. Do you intend patronising the officers theatricals ?" he added, turning to Miss Lawrence.

Before that young lady could answer, Mrs. Grainger burst in with—

" Surely they winna do anything sae fule-like."

" The evening for the performance is fixed," continued Ernest. " The proceeds are, I understand to be appropriated to the poor."

" They'd muckle better gie it to our charitable fund," said Mrs. Grainger, " ye'll excuse me, Mr. Basil, but I maunna alloo your visit to mak me neglec my duties. Reach me yon bit bookie Constance ; this 'll no be one of my

heaviest day's I'm thinkin," and she ran over
a memorandum containing her appointments.
"Schule at three, missionary meeting at four,
charitable association at five, tea at six. Mr.
Mucklewhackit's lecture at seven."

"And this is one of your light days Mrs.
Grainger," said Miss Lawrence. "Dear me,
I should think it heavy enough. How can you
support so many fatiguing engagements."

"In the *purshuit* of duty we maunna tire,"
said Mrs. Grainger, adding piously, "*He* wha
tempers the wind to the shorn lambie, aye suits
the back to the burthen. Mr. Basil, ye'll say
to yere mither that I'll try and overtake her
sune when I'm na sae fashed as at the present
speaking. Gin Mistress Basil and yoursel'
wad *jist* wave a' ceremony and tak your tea
wi' us to-morrow evening, me and Mr.
Grainger expec a few friens, na much company,
just a few friens."

"I shall not fail to report your kind invitation to Mrs. Basil," said Ernest, "and will
undertake to say that ceremony would not keep

her away, but I know she has an engagement for to-morrow evening. I however have none, and will have great pleasure in making one of your party."

"Miss Constance, if you are ready for a walk, we will all go out together," said Miss Lawrence.

Ernest retired from this much dreaded interview with a heart. considerably lightened. He had at length ventured—

> "To beard the lion in his den,
> The Douglas in his hall."

He had been introduced to Mrs. Grainger, and had survived the interview, and even turned it to advantage, for he had come off with flying colours, and an invitation to a Free Church converzazione. Moreover, Mrs. Grainger had graciously permitted Constance to take another sitting. There was she and Miss Lawrence, and himself, all in the street together.

"Well, you certainly have achieved a miracle to get an invitation out of Mrs. Grainger, and on such short notice," said Miss Fairweather. " How glad I am you're coming, aren't you Elinor. Her parties are all so tiresome; a lot of stupid clergymen, and just enough of young men to make one feel the restraint. Alec. Flaccid calls them " *muffin-worries.*" Yet it is selfish in me to wish you to spend a dull evening."

" How can I spend a dull evening if Miss Fairweather is present," said Ernest, with more *empressement* than he usually infused into his every-day compliments. " I declare I feel so happy this morning, as if I could forgive anybody, as if I loved Mrs. Grainger and the whole world. What can be the reason."

" It must be the fine weather," said Miss Fairweather ; " and yet don't you think it looks like rain ?"

" Rain indeed, nonsense, it can't rain, it shan't rain—I mean it won't. Why it is the most beautiful day for a walk, and I was just going to propose one down on the sands by the sea shore."

" Do you think we dare go, Elinor," said Miss Fairweather.

" To be sure ; why not," said Miss Lawrence. " We will be as safe with Mr. Basil there as in his studio, and Mrs. Grainger will be engrossed with the " Borryoboolagha" duties all the afternoon."

But Miss Lawrence concealed a design under her evident desire to promote this walk. She was too quick-sighted not to see that Mr. Basil's attentions were levelled entirely at her friend, and she had no idea of making a party of three to stroll on the sands. Just as they were getting clear of the town, she exclaimed—

" Now I am really sorry to break up such a happy party, but I have promissed so often to call upon my good old friend, Mrs. M'Clure, that I dare not go past her house. Yonder sits the good old lady at the window with her knitting. You two go on and enjoy your walk, and take me up as you pass. I shall be on the look out even if you should forget my existence. Good bye, I hope you won't miss me very much," cried the laughing, beautiful girl as she waved an adieu from the steps in front of Mrs. M'Clure's door.

Ernest was not so much engrossed by Miss Fairweather, that he did not thoroughly appreciate this goodnatured manœuvre on Miss Lawrence's part, and felt so grateful to her in consequence, that just then, if he had not loved Constance he might have loved Elinor.

Few young men, we presume, walk with young ladies alone, especially by the sea side, without either making love or thinking of making it; and when it is in the thoughts, it comes so naturally to the lips, even if those tell-tales, the eyes, have not already discovered it. The French say, talking of love is making it. We also say that we may be doing our very best to inspire love when we are neither thinking nor talking about it.

In pleasant converse the time wore quickly away, and even the lovers, if we may be allowed to style them such, began at last to think of returning and relieving Miss Lawrence

from her self-imposed duty of watching for
them at Mrs. M'Clure's window. Whatever
that kind hearted young lady thought, she did
not either by word or look manifest the slightest impatience.

CHAPTER IX.

MRS. GRAINGER'S CONVERSAZIONE.

On the memorable evening in question
Ernest having got himself up with infinitely
more care and attention than he had been in
the habit lately of bestowing on his toilette,
knocked at Mrs. Grainger's door and was duly
ushered into the assemblage of materials for
sociability which that good lady had collected
in her drawing-room. At first there was but a
vague impression of being surrounded by sundry
gentlemen in black coats and white cravats, by
no means remarkable for the brilliancy and
vivacity of their appearance; a due proportion
of elderly ladies of every variety of aspect,
vinegar predominating, and a fair sprinkling of
young ones, which formed the redeeming points
of the landscape. The party seemed to be
indeed one of these irreverently, but signifi-
cantly, termed by Flaccid " *muffin worries.*"

It was a judicious or injudicious (?) assemblage of distinctions in age, sex, and congeniality; of parties in no respect assimilating with one another, and forming, consequently, a conglomeration, better adapted to afford opportunities of studying character, than for any specific method of beguiling the rosy hours. The young and the old did not mix or blend together. The young people sitting apart listless and sighing for some more decided relaxation than a little desultory conversation and an occasional song, for Mrs. Grainger would as soon have thought of bending the knee to Moloch or setting up Juggernaut or Vishu for her guests to worship, as permitting cards or dancing.

In attempting to convey to the reader some idea of a Free Church converzazione, it would be unpardonable to omit several clergymen, the first in importance, if not in picturesque appearance. At the first general view they might not appear as adding materially to the sociability of the evening as they seemed neither ornamental nor useful, making no efforts to amuse or be amused, but standing about the room in ungainly attitudes as if their mission had been (which perhaps it was) to act as dampers on the too general flow of hilarity which might else have burst beyond the proper limits of Free Church decorum. Nevertheless we will attempt to enter somewhat more into detail in our description of these "*dear men.*"

The first in peace, first in the pulpit (certainly not in war) and the first in the hearts of his congregation, also the first in physical, if not in intellectual magnitude was the Rev. Saunders Mucklewhackit, a large clumsy, ill-built, ill-looking man, who stood bolt-upright before the fire-place, looking very much like a master of the house, too surly to speak to his guests. (as Mr. Grainger was only the nominal master of the house and plays no part in our story, it is not necessary to introduce him personally to the reader). The Rev. Mr. Mucklewhackit, resembled a particularly surly mastiff, whose good qualities can only be appreciated by those who are sufficiently acquainted with him to forget the roughness of his exterior. He possessed a certain amount of shrewdness and ability, which was magnified by his own sect, into little short of *Nestorian* wisdom, for narrow-minded, one-sided men frequently impose upon their admirers by the energy and determination with which they embrace views, and utter opinions, where abler men would suspend their judgement. A rugged fluency of language was considered eloquence, and Mr. Mucklewhackit was esteemed by the Free Church people of Y——, an orator hardly inferior to Demosthenes ; a reputation undiminished by his broad provincial dialect and ungainly gesticulation, and not to be wondered at, when it is recollected that few of those who sat under him. had ever heard a good English speaker, either of the bar or pulpit.

Mr. Mucklewhackit, if he had not found ample food for his love of adulation in the ministry, would have been the leader of a party, or a demagogue in some other shape or way.

He had, indeed, tried both law and trade before he bestowed his talents on the church. He was one of those who sailed with the times, and by judiciously siding with the most popular party and " by apostatising at the right time," gratified his own love of notoriety, and feathered his nest at one and the same time. He had gone over to the Free Church with a great pomp of conscientious avowal when the Free Church seemed likely to supplant the established Kirk of Scotland, and now in his zeal, goes beyond the Emperor of China, who after having *dined, permits*, but does not *force*, all the world to go to dinner. But when Mr. Mucklewhackit has changed his views he will have every one else do so likewise, and everybody under pain of his displeasure must confess the superiority of the Free over the Established Church. Mr. Mucklewhackit used to like several glasses of toddy at a sitting, but the temperance movement came in, and Mr. Mucklewhackit found his account in joining it, and has ever since preached against the *poor labourer* who refreshes himself occasionally with the national beverage. As for the *rich,* who can drink wine and spirits with impunity because they can afford to import them in large quantities, Mr. Mucklewhackit *takes care to let them alone.* As a perfectly good man is not to be found, it may be observed, that there is one of the cardinal virtues at least, in which Mr. Mucklewhackit is deficient, and that is courage. This, Ernest had an opportunity of remarking while crossing the ferry in a small boat along with the minister. Mr. Mucklewhackit, on that occasion, grasped the sides of the boat nervously, and desired an adventurous passenger to sit down, with a good deal of unction and an ejaculation, which savoured more of personal fear than prayer.

" Deil tak ye, canna ye sit down mon, wha ever *hard of* standing up in a flat-bottomed boat that has na hold on the water."

The boatman, a shrewd highlander, when they had reached the opposite side, observed

Ernest looking after the minister, and answered to the expression on his face rather than to any verbal remark—

" Your honor ull be thinkin the minister dreadfu' feart o' the water."

" It did strike me as strange, friend, that one whose business it is to prepare man for death, should show such a terror of it himself.'

" Deed, and that's a wise-like remark, and whiles I'm thinkin sae mysel', but one maunna jist be ower hard upon folk o' a peacefu trade like the ministry. A weel, a wat, it's a' habit, thae wha are na ca'd to gang down till the sea in ships and occupy their bizness in great waters, maun jist be excusit for bein a we timersome about droonin."

Mr. Mucklewhackit, take him for all in all, is not a bad sort of a man. He only believes that inasmuch as Scotland is the greatest country in the world, and owes its superiority to the Free Church, of which he is one of the most useful (certainly not most ornamental) pillars, he himself stands a little before Socrates

Seneca, Luther, John Knox, and a host of celebrated philosophers and reformers.

Ernest was introduced by Mrs. Grainger to Mr. Mucklewhackit as though his favour and countenance were most essential to her guest.

" I'm jist vera sorry we're no to have your mither's society. Mr. Mucklewhackit this 'ill be Maister Basil, son of Mrs. Basil. Maybe you'll mind her lang syne."

Mr. Mucklewhackit, whose abruptness savoured of rudeness, turned upon Ernest immediately, with the query. " How's your mother ?" probably not aware that he was making use of a slang enquiry of the period.

" Mrs. Basil is tolerably well," said Ernest coldly.

" And you'll be frae America, Mr. Basil ? You'll find Y—— a fine place compared with your America towns, which are built of wood as I've *hard*, and where the cattle and the pigs run about the streets."

Ernest merely bowed, and one or two elderly ladies to whom every word that the minister said, both in and out of the pulpit, was gospel, drew a long breath and muttered an audible " Eh sirs !"

Mr. Mucklewhackit having found an audience, went on. " The want of comfort, the rudeness of manners in the people, might be borne, but the extremes of heat and cold arc, I have *hard* intolerable. Strokes of the sun are every-day occurrences in summer, and in winter it is quite common for one person to stop and rub another person's nose with a handful of snow to remedy the effects of frost."

" Which fully accounts," said Ernest, " for all Americans dying at thirty, for they're being so fond of sherry-cobblers, and other cooling drinks in summer, and for a large portion of the British colonists going by the name of *blue noses.*"

" Eh, but yon's *fearful,*" said an old lady from the Highlands, " yon maun be an awfu' country to bide in amang savages and sic like folk."

The Rev. Dr. Dottlewit was a character very

dissimilar to Mr. Mucklewhackit.   He was a
man of considerable ability and erudition, and
had originally held a chair in the university of
Edinbugh, which his growing infirmity of absence of mind compelled him to vacate.   He
appeared generally not to have the most remote
consciousness of what was going on or where
he was, and only now and then plunged into
the conversation at a venture, with some disjointed remarks, generally on religious subjects,
which made it difficult (from the incongruity
both in time and place) for strangers to preserve their gravity.   Alec Flaccid was causing
a good deal of tittering in one corner by a re-
hearsal of some of the good doctor's peculiarities, while the Rev. gentleman himself, who
had been hitherto ruminating placidly over a
" bap" and a cup of coffee beside Ernest, whom
he had not noticed when introduced half an hour
previously, suddenly broke the silence with the
following remark—

" I trust, Mr. Basil, you dinna neglect the
one thing needful.   I hope you are fully alive

to the necessity of striving to save ourselves
from the gulph which is yawning to receive our
sinful souls, and convinced that we are utterly
powerless of ourselves to do anything of the
sort ?"

" I try and do my duty," Ernest was beginning, when the doctor taking another
mouthful of the " bap," cut him short—

" All of no avail—works without faith ; only
one way, Mr. Basil : through His blood. You
have been in Edinburgh, Mr. Basil, I am sorry
I did not see you then. I should have had
time to discuss those matters with you. I leave
Y—— to-morrow."

" But I hope to be in Edinburgh in the
winter, and then I shall not fail to call."

The worthy doctor's eyes brightened at this
hope. He shook Ernest heartily by the hand,
begged him not to fail to call when he came
to Edinburgh, assured him he would devote hours
—days, if necessary—to enlighten him upon
the means of salvation, and then began another
" bap" and seemed wholly unconscious of Ernest's

existence, or the presence of any living being
in the room. After tea the clergymen went
away with the exception of one young man,
the Rev. Mr. Fleech, who was very fond of
young ladies' society, and who, according to
Flaccid, had jilted several who had not been
able to resist his eloquence and his personal
attractions combined, in the pulpit. No sooner
had Mr. Mucklewhackit disappeared than the
seniors were loud in his praises. His kindness and condescension in " coming in till his
tea just like any other body," were much lauded,
and it was carried *nem. con.* that he was just a
" *dear man.*" The young ladies appeared to
think that a young clergyman in hand was
worth any quantity of old ones *absent,* and the
Misses Flaccid in particular began courting
his attention, for it was pretty well known that
Mr. Fleech was on the look out for a wife to
do the honors of his manse. Ernest's attention was now drawn to an animated discussion
carried on by a knot of elderly ladies on a
melancholy event which had just occurred in

Y——. Every town has besides its *"good young man,"* its wild graceless scamps, who set all order and decorum at defiance, and seem bent on going headlong to ruin. One of these had just come to an untimely end, yet one which his mad career had all along foreboded. He had been found drowned in the river, and there was too much reason to fear that he had made away with himself.

Miss Becky Scunnerweel, had she been a man would have found more happiness in the life of a Bedouin Arab than ought else. Her tongue, if not her hand, was not only against every man, but also against every woman and child who came within the sphere of her observation. Partly from idiosyncrasy, partly from the result of her position, an old maid, standing aloof from the busy world around, seeing displayed before her eyes domestic enjoyments, in which she has no participation, no sympathy, with none of those ties which married people possess, with no daily toil to sweeten life—she had grown a pariah, an outcast from society, and revenged upon the world, as far as she could, the injuries she had received from it.   Having no business of her own to attend to, she naturally interfered as much as possible with the affairs of others.   And who can blame her if, without the domestic resources of other women—without superior abilities to enable her to soar above the every-day world, to find a refuge in literature and other abstract studies—and without *work*, that boon which makes the mischief of celibacy disappear comparatively in the lower classes—poor Miss Scunnerweel should be a mischievous idler, gadding about from house to house to receive and retail scandal, and generally feared as a busy-body and a newsmonger?

"Of course ye'll aw have *hard*," said Miss Scunnerweel, "about Sandy Murdoch's death?"

"Indeed, and indeed," said Mrs. Wearygab, "it was what might hae been weel expeckit. Did I no say," she continued, turning appealingly to Mrs. Grainger, "that yon laddie was ganging till perdition, aften I hae ken't him

gae past our house at twal o' the day in-
toxicate to that degree, that it was just *fe-a-rful*
to witness."

" Ou, aye," said Miss Scunnerweel, who
seemed ever willing to differ from the last
speaker, " there's mony ane to say noo that
the chiel's dead, I aye tell't ye it wad be sae.
More shame they didna' fash themselves, when
they might hae saved baith saul and bodie."

Mrs. Wearygab, who thought this taunt
particularly levelled at her, was bridling up to
return the compliment, when Mrs. Grainger
threw a new light on the subject by saying—

" And what'll become o' the lassie, Jeannie
Armstrong, and she engaged to him as I ken
weel she has been a gay while, spite o' his
headstrang ways ?"

" It's a grand pity they were na just married
afore the puir body drowned himsel'."

" Aye, and what then ?" said Miss Scunner-
well.

" Do ye no see in yon case the bit property which he has na quite dissipated a'thegither would hae been hers?"

"And wha has a better right to the bit property," said Miss Scunnerweel, with a glance of great scorn at Mrs. Wearygab, "wha has a better right to the bit property, and she engaged to be married to him. She'll get it now, I trow, without the encumbrance."

"Surely," said Ernest, joining in because he felt it impossible to be silent any longer, "if she is not an utterly worthless, heartless girl, she is thinking of something else at this moment, when her lover is lying dead, than some miserable property." But all the ladies now joined together and bore down upon him to prove that Jeannie Armstrong would and should have the bit property, that no one had a better right to it, &c.

"And what'll they do wi' him, puir laddie? They canna jist bury him like ony ither body, ye ken?"

Miss Scunnerweel would probably have been as indignant as anyone else if it had been proposed to give poor Alexander Murdoch Christian burial, but true to her principle of dissenting from Mrs. Wearygab, she immediately retorted—

" Bring it home to your ain sel' : if any of your friends or acquaintance, forbye relatives, had drowned themsel's, how wad ye like the minister to refuse them Christian burial ?"

" Friends or nae friends," said Mrs. Grainger, " ye'll nae catch Mr. Mucklewhackit, or any other respeckit minister, attending the burial o' Alexander Murdoch or any ither body wha makes awa' wi' himsel'."

" Weel, I wadna like to be Mr. Mucklewhackit, to refuse the laddie's friends," said Miss Scunnerweel.

Ernest had heard quite enough to satisfy him of the depth of *philanthropy* and *Christianity* of Mrs. Grainger and her friends.

CHAPTER X.

THE attention of the company was now directed to a song.   The eldest Miss Flaccid had
been prevailed upon to sing. The three Misses
Flaccids were, as we have already said, model
young ladies.   They go to church on Sundays
with their bonnets half on their heads, to confess themselves miserable sinners, and then
return to fill up the measure of their wicked-
ness during the week with shopping, crozier-
ing, pic-nics, and dances.   They are not particularly fond of reading, though they own, of
course, to Scott's and Cooper's novels, and they
believe to a great extent in Uncle Tom's Cabin,
also that the world is round; but if you were
to ask them what causes night and day, and
the changes of the seasons, they would be puz-
zled to answer.   They have heard that Galileo

discovered *something*, and know that Columbus discovered America. They are very fond of " *work*" in the sense in which young ladies understand it, and they multiply varieties of patterns of crochet to cover the backs of sofas and arm-chairs, and make wonderful little nondescript baskets, &c., which can be put to no imaginable use, typical of an idle, useless existence. Their conversation is generally on local topics, about the bonnet worn by Brigadier Blazer's lady at church, whether Miss Young will really come out at the next assembly, and whether Ensign Spark will really marry Miss Gadd. Mrs. Flaccid boasts that that she knows every thought in her daughters' heads, and she may do so without possessing any very original ideas. Of one thing we may be sure, that the Misses Flaccid would never have a thought that was *outré* or odd. Propriety is written on every line of their countenances, it lurks in the braids of their hair, in the primness of their pursed-up mouths, and may be discovered in their very waists, narrowed to the exact measurement recognised as the improvement of art over nature. We cannot call the Misses Flaccid young women, nor do they appear ever to have been girls. They are *young ladies*, and to a man who has still a chord responsive to nature left in his bosom, are thoroughly insipid. There is no occasion to individualise them—they are all alike. They will laugh, chat, coquet, and polka through their allotted number of seasons, laying traps with the proper degree of secresy for eligible husbands. None of them will be influenced by such an incumbrance as a heart and feelings in determining her choice. Manly beauty, manly intellect, and manly worth will pass before them undiscovered, uncomprehended, and disregarded, and when each has succeeded in hooking the man sufficiently well off in worldly gear to be an eligible *parti*, each will display the same becoming amount of maidenly astonishment, and perturbation, and physical depression at the proposal which she has waited, angled, dressed, and danced for so long.

Miss Flaccid, on being asked to sing, was sure that she had no voice, (in which, by the bye, she was quite correct) then, that she had a cold, and that she really couldn't; whereupon everybody in the immediate neighbourhood declared that Miss Flaccid's singing would make them *so happy*, and Miss Flaccid, either from not being proof against so general a desire of happiness, or thinking that she had been pressed sufficiently, and that she had better sing while she had the opportunity, hemmed the proper number of times, and began. Her singing was really miraculous in one sense, for she really had no voice in the sense in which vocalists are said to possess a voice. She sang without feeling, taste, expression, or harmony, just the sort of song through which everybody talks, and at the close of which everybody says thank you, neither knowing nor caring what the song is about, with perhaps a feeling of gratitude to the young lady who has been thumping the piano and murmuring in cadence for the last

thirty minutes, under cover of which conversations and flirtations have been going merrily
on, for Miss Flaccid's singing had this recom-
mendation, that she did not force the attention
by screaming. Her song, when ended, left you
under a pleasing uncertainty as to the nature
and subject both of words and music. It
might have been grave or gay, a lament or a
roundelay. Ernest was endeavouring to imagine whether it was the prayer from Norma or
" Rob Roy M'Gregor O," when Miss Bayard
observed—" A nice soft voice." The young
ladies could afford to praise Miss Flaccid.

Then Miss Greenshields sat down to the
piano, and sang what Ernest thought a sweet
pretty little song, all about wandering on the
sea shore and picking up shells. He liked
both music and words ; indeed, there was a
vein of philosophy about the latter which particularly pleased him—

> Oh thus, I said, in every age
>   By toys our fancy is beguiled,
> We gather shells from youth to age,
>   And then we leave them like a child.

Miss Flaccid thought the words pretty, but could not agree as to the execution ; she had heard it much better sung. Miss Fairweather was then requested to sing, but declined, on the plea of not being equal to it that evening. And Ernest was not sorry, he wished her to sing for him alone, that his ears only might drink in the melody, and no voice but his might whisper praise.

"Does not Miss Blair sing ?" said Ernest to Miss Flaccid. That young lady looked surprised—

"Is it possible you have never heard Miss Blair sing ?"

"No, indeed ; I hope she will to-night."

"Oh, she'll sing fast enough, never fear ; she's only waiting to be asked."

The mystery of this reply was soon solved. Miss Blair was such a singer as is seldom met with among amateurs. She had indeed received a careful musical education, and possessed powers of voice which many a professional singer might have envied. Ernest could not help remarking that few or no young ladies asked Miss Blair to sing. She possessed such an acknowledged superiority, that no one could venture to sing after her with any effect. Consequently she generally remained mistress of the instrument when she sat down to it. If she seemed to enjoy her triumph over the little feelings of envy and jealousy, Ernest thought there was some good excuse for it.

" She does not seem to require much pressing," said he to Miss Flaccid, noticing the alacrity with which Miss Blair complied with his request to sing, and moved to the piano.

" That's because she knows she can do it so well, you know. She's quite aware she's above all criticism."

Here the full rich voice of Miss Blair swelled out in the air of " *Come e gentil*," and Ernest was wafted into the seventh heaven of imagination. Not that he thought it superior to Miss Fairweather's when he came to criticise it coolly after the song had ceased. No; Miss Blair's

voice might be richer, but she certainly was
inferior in expression to Miss Fairweather.
But while she was singing he was looking at
Constance and building castles in the air with
his usual celerity. Music certainly is an ac-
complishment, or rather let us call it a divine
gift, which draws the heart more immediately
towards its possessor than either poetry or
painting. When a beautiful woman is singing, a man of imagination is inclined to prostrate himself before her as a goddess. We
may even forget the poet or the painter in
the contemplation of their works, but who can
disconnect that glorious harmony from the
mortal being who is producing it, while our
spirits are thrilling, even now thrilling under
its influence. The effect of music is more
instantaneous, general, and independent of
previous education than that of any other art.
As a well known author eloquently remarks—
" One blast of her trumpet, and thousands
rush forth to die—one peal of her organ, and
millions kneel down to pray."

The song ceases, and the goddess of our imagination becomes again an ordinary young lady.

"How delightful it must be to you to sing in the soft Italian," said Ernest to Miss Blair, "having once heard it sung, all other languages seem harsh. How I envy you the privilege of reading Dante and Petrarch too in the original."

"Bless you," said Miss Blair, very frankly, "I don't understand the meaning of the words; I only learn how to pronounce them so that I can sing them. It is so unfashionable not to sing Italian."

"Honest, at least," thought Ernest to himself, though he felt he never could listen to an Italian song from Miss Blair again with the same interest as when he fancied she understood the meaning of the words she poured out so sweetly.

"Now that you have heard Miss Blair sing, you will not wonder that she requires no pressing, and that no one has to ask her twice."

" Why, Miss Flaccid, how you are praising
Miss Blair," said Miss Hilaire, a lively young
lady who had lately returned from a visit to
Paris, and whose clear ringing laugh sounded
like an alarm to mirth.... " Don't you know
that is what all gentlemen admire so much in
a young lady, to sing when she is asked? I
am sure I always try to please that way. I
only wish some one had asked me to sing before Miss Blair." ..

" I hope it is not too late now," said Ernest,
" to make good your assertion that you always
sing when you are asked ?"

" But indeed it is !" said Miss Hilaire,
laughing, " for I am as obstinate as regards
the exception as the rule itself. No one who
is wise will sing after Miss Blair."

" Preserve us," cried Mrs. Wearygab from
the other side of the room, where the elder
ladies sat in solemn conclave round Mrs.
Grainger, conversing chiefly on religious topics,
and comparing the merits of their several
preachers, seasoned occasionally with some pi-

quant sauce in the shape of scandal, " if that's
no yon Miss Hilaire laughing again. My head's
fairly like to split when once she begins. It's
really no proper for young ladies to laugh in
sic a boisterous like manner."

The old Highland lady, before alluded to,
shook her head, enveloped in an enormously
high cap, made after some antiquated fashion
long out of date, and delivered herself of the
following oracular sentence—

. " Gin young leddies gang till Pairis, out
ower the channel, to learn sic manners, I
hope none o' my bairns, or my bairn's bairns,
will ever pit fit out o' bonnie Scotland !"

Which sentiment, enforced with a pinch of
snuff, met with general approval.

" Do you think Miss Hilaire's light-heart-
edness such a crime ?" said Ernest to Miss
Lawrence, who happened to be next him at
the moment. " I am sure I have often felt
indebted to her for her merry cheerful laugh
at parties when I should otherwise have sank
into a state of abject despondency. I only

wish we had a few more that could laugh like her in Y——. 1 feel most grateful to her when she laughs, and am always ready to join her without wanting to know the cause."

" But is it not amazing," said Miss Lawrence, " to note the difference which age and habit make in people's opinions. The very thing you like in Miss Hilaire, her hearty laugh, these good ladies disapprove of "——

" It is certainly natural," said Ernest, " that old people should think differently from young, and that their nerves should be shaken by that which is only agreeable excitement to us ; but still you must admit that old and young should yield somewhat to each other, and thus enjoy themselves, as far as possible, in common, or else form separate assemblages. I have been watching pretty closely this evening, and it appears to me that neither seniors nor juniors have been so happy as they might have been, and that they seem rather inclined to be critical on each other. When we hear those whose years

should have taught them some forbearance ob-
jecting to a young lady for a harmless laugh "—

" And when Mr. Basil philosophises so
cooly on the conduct of his seniors."

" Very good, Miss Lawrence, but not my
" masters, nor pastors, nor those who are placed
in authority over me." I was only taking up
the cudgels in defence of the young people.
Here are a number of them expected to find
amusement in the same sedentary occupation
of the elders, viz., tea and "——

" Go on, out with it, Mr. Basil. Shall I
finish the sentence for you—tea and scandal."

" It is your own addition, Miss Lawrence—
tea and toast."

" No, that won't do, Mr. Basil, we have had
no toast to-night. Nothing is fashionable but
cakes of all descriptions."

" But you make no allowance for alliteration
and poetical license. Tea, and toast, and scandal, if you insist upon it. But do you not
think that a party of this kind is a failure—

.that it pleases neither young nor old? I'll wager that neither you, nor I, nor the Misses Flaccid care to know into how many heads Mr. Mucklewhackit's last discourse was divided, which Mrs. Grainger is now enumerating, and to be told over and over again that he is a dear man."

Miss Lawrence laughed, and Miss Hilaire positively rang the changes on the vowels.

" Lord ha' a care o' us, but I'm fairly deaved wi' yon lassie," cried the unfortunate lady with the head. Ernest continued —

" Now contrast this with another sort of evening. At a certain house, at a certain hour, certain elderly ladies will be observed either walking up, carrying their cap baskets in their hand, or alighting from their cabs. Then after tea there is a game at quadrille or whist for the elders, while the young people amuse themselves with speculation, or commerce, or music. Then comes the cosy supper, and the chat, perhaps a song, over a very moderate modicum of toddy, and then the good old

steady polite cab driver, who is making a fortune out of such regular customers, takes them
back to their own homes, and all the dissipation will be over, and they will be snug in bed
by eleven at the outside. Now there's nothing
very cynical in what I am saying."

"Oh, no, you are not a cynic now, but quite
a good-natured critic. You must admit, Mr.
Basil, that though you hate Y—— "—

"My dear Miss Lawrence, how do you know
I hate it?"

"Oh, I know very well what you used to
think of it, although perhaps your feelings
may have undergone a change lately from some
cause or other. Now you won't interrupt me
again," said Miss Lawrence, with something
like a wicked smile flitting over her beautiful
features, "but to continue, now that you are
listening so attentively, you must admit that
Y—— is a fine field for a philosopher like
yourself to study character in, and that you will
carry away many new lights upon propriety and
decorum, and matters, and things in general.

I do believe if poor dear Mrs. Grainger were
to know you as well as I do, your ideas, political and social, and all your innovating agitating doctrines, she could not sleep with the
idea that she had been under the same roof
with so dangerous a person, with so odd a
young man."

" Thank you, Miss Lawrence, for my character," said Ernest, laughing. " I certainly
have increased my knowledge of character considerably, though not to the increase of my
contentment always. But what sound is that ?"

" It is a street organ, and very nicely played
by a woman; I know the sound of her organ, it
is so superior to all the rest."

" Oh yes, that German woman with the little
girl who beats the tambourine; I have given
her many a penny. I discover signs of com-
motion among Mrs. Grainger's circle already."

The music now approached so near the window as to be distinctly audible and it was amusing to watch the variety of effect it occasioned.
While some of the young ladies beat time de-

lighted to a merry polka, several of the elderly
ladies displayed symptoms of discontent and
vexation at the cheerful sounds. Mrs. Grainger
rang the bell violently, and said to the servant
who answered it.

"Betty you'll gang out and send awa yon
huzzie wi' a flee in her lug."

Betty withdrew, and the result of her mission
was soon apparent in the sudden stoppage of a
lively polka, and the blank expression which
revisited the countenances of some of the youth-
ful listeners.

Ernest and Miss Lawrence glanced involun-
tarily at each other as much as to say now for it.
"What a disgrace for a woman to wander aboot
in yon idle vagrant way, instead of makin' an
honest wise-like living with work," said Mrs.
Grainger.

"I wud ha' sich huzzies publicly scourged,"
said Miss Scunnerweel, and similar remarks
passed from mouth to mouth.

Whether out of a malicious desire to stir up
a hornet's nest about his ears, or because he

really felt indignant at hearing such unjust and disparaging remarks against the *idleness* of the poor music-grinder from a party of ladies who had done nothing for several hours but talk scandal of their neighbours, we know not, but Ernest made an observation which called down the collected wrath of all the elders on his devoted head.

" Perhaps the woman prefers this method of making a livelihood either to washing or mangling."

Cruickshank alone could have conveyed the looks of mingled amazement and horror from the senior portion, and the mischevious, partially concealed mirth of the junior part of the company at the unheard of proposition of a woman in her walk of life, presuming to have an opinion of her own, or preferring one species of labour to another. Some stared in speechless wonder at the atrocity of the principles conveyed in such a speech, others darted looks of fiery indignation which should have annihilated Ernest on the spot, and the remainder shook

their heads with a sort of pitying patronising
air as much as to say " we maunna won'er at
anything from sic à quarter."

Ernest felt the spirit of a martyr rising within
him.   He had gone too far to retreat.

" And why should not the poor person have
a choice of livelihood as well as those above
her in station.   Is poverty to have no rights,
no privileges.   A lady or gentleman, may kill
time, may be as idle and useless as they choose.
A young nobleman may lounge away a whole
morning at his club, an ensign in country
quarters may perambulate the streets, staring
modest girls out of countenance or spit over a
bridge for hours, and neither be accused of
being a disgrace to society.   But for the poor
woman disabled perhaps by physical debility,
from gaining a livelihood in another manner (he
thought he would make out as strong a case as
possible) who is infringing no law, who sends a
gleam of enjoyment to the heart of all the poor
children in the streets she visits, there is
nothing but censure."

"Well I do like Mr. Basil for speaking out so honestly and I think it quite true every word he says," whispered Miss Hilaire to Miss Lawrence.

"Don't you think Mr. Basil says very odd things," said Miss Flaccid to another young lady. "I never met in with a young man so odd or who talks like him, before."

"You are quite right," said Miss Lawrence, with an irony which Miss Flaccid did not appreciate, "Mr. Basil is very different from other young men, certainly as far as my experience goes."

"And wha will yon Maister Basil be," said the old Highland lady, "wha taks sae muckle on himself. A painter," said the old lady whose ideas immediately reverted to visions of ladders, white lead, and house painting "ye dinna mean to tell me that Mrs. Grainger wud hae askit me to meet wi' a painter." Her Highland blood was somewhat cooled by the explanation of the word; but still she was far from being reconciled to Mr. Basil or his profession.

"A portrait painter frae America, my certie. He's a camsteary chiel to set up wi' his gab that gate afore folk sae muckle aulder and wiser. The warld's at a pretty come-to-pass, when a lad educate in thae outlandish countries where there's naething but savages and wild beasties is sae glib on a' subject. I wuss he maunna hae dethical (deistical) principles, but I'se na like to answer for him wi' his new-fangled notions. It canna be expected that ane brought up in thae far awa wilderness countries can hae the moral and releegious training o' the youth o' Scotlan'."

"And that's a maist sensible observe o' yours, Mrs. Clishmaclaver," said Mrs. Weary-ga'. "I rede ye tak tent o' Maister Close wha iver hard him setting up wi' sic idle clashes. Mony, and mony's the evening ye'll no hear him spak word good nor bad, and I ken weel its no in's head nor heart to devise any sic oreeginal and republican principles; but, indeed, there'll be few to compare till him for douce, wise-like behaviour. We aw ken Mrs.

Grainger, he's just a pattern to the rising generation and a credit to the kirk. I wad as soon expect to see the pu'pit wanten Mr. Mucklewhackit as to ken Maister Close absent frae the twa services. Odd, but it does my heart gude to hear him skirlin up the psalm."

Alic Flaccid had in the meantime been endeavouring to make himself agreeable in his usual way by a repetition of ancedotes generally having reference to parties present. He had told a number of stories about Mr. Mucklewhackit and Dr. Dottlewit, some of which, whether founded on fact or imagination, were ludicrous enough. According to him, Mr. Mucklewhackit had on one occasion given a very *striking* proof of his zeal in the pulpit. One of the congregation, a devout man, wishing to shut out every object which might by any chance withdraw his thoughts from the chapter in the bible which the minister was reading, had covered his eyes with his hands, and presented to an ordinary observer the appearance of being fast asleep, though in reality, not losing a word.   In an unlucky moment for him, the minister's eye fell upon this seemingly careless disciple, and, fired with wrath at what he imagined so deliberate a breach of propriety, he took deliberate aim at the defaulter with the bible which he had been reading, crying out as the missile left his hand with fatal accuracy— " Odd mon gin ye winna hear the word of God, I'se mak ye feel it."

Miss Hilaire laughed so long and so loud at this anecdote, that Mrs. Wearygab, as she expressed it, could thole it no longer ; and her abrupt rising proved the signal for a general break up, and thus terminated Ernest's first experience of a Free Church converzazione.

CHAPTER XI.

THE limits of Miss Fairweather's sojourn in
Y——, began to draw so very near, that
Ernest felt if he would speak at all he must
speak quickly. Such was the thought which
occupied his mind while listening to the bewitching melody of Miss Fairweather's voice
one evening she spent at his mother's but
a few days before that fixed on for her departure.
On this occasion she seemed more lovely, more
enchanting, more engaging than ever. Miss
Fairweather had evidently perceived his admiration, and seemed willing to heighten it as far
as possible on this evening by appearing to the
utmost possible advantage. She sang all his
favourite songs to-night as if by intuition.
What a witch—what an *abandon* there is
about a lovely woman's singing to her lover.

Every word, every emphasis, every inflection of the voice is pregnant with feeling. When she burst out in a full tide of harmony in that exquisite air, and in those exquisite words—

> Still so gently o'er me stealing,
> Mem'ry will bring back the feeling,
> Spite of all my griefs revealing,
> That I love thee, love thee still.

Ernest felt that it was useless to contend against the feelings of intense admiration—sincere and ardent love with which his heart was embued towards Miss Fairweather. He might have knelt and worshipped her, but for the presence of Mrs. Basil ; and was this fair being to depart from Y—— without hearing from his own lips how he loved her. That she had perceived his manifest admiration he could not doubt. Her willingness to accept invitations to the house, the evident pleasure which she took in his company, proved it; but how can we read one another's thoughts ? She might at this moment be endeavouring to steel her heart against one whom she deemed a mere capricious, inconstant admirer. For what proof had he given of the fervor and sincerity of his affection. And this might be the last night he should ever have such an opportunity. Why then, not to-night? Why should he shrink another moment from avowing his first, his honest single-hearted preference of her to all others? Yes, it should be so. He mentally vowed to-night he would learn his fate; better to be a rejected suiter now than to let the feeling, which every day gathered weight, grow utterly beyond the power of control.

"Let us go home by the sands to night Miss Fairweather, do, as a favour, we may never again have such another opportunity. It is still early and there is a glorious moon."

Miss Fairweather appeared to hesitate a little.

"Mrs. Grainger is spending the evening out to night, if I thought I would be home before she returned." With this protest she suffered Ernest to draw her arm within his and direct her towards the place he had mentioned.

Miss Fairweather appeared in excellent

spirits this evening, indeed, too much so, as
Ernest thought, for what he had to say. He
would have been better pleased had he discerned
more sentiment in her manner.

" And what is this important secret which
you say you have to tell me," said Miss Fairweather, in a lively tone, which nevertheless
Ernest thought was assumed to veil serious
curiosity. He did not answer at first, his heart
was plunged into that turmoil of hopes and
fears, which can be imagined to occupy a *lover*
on the eve of such an important communication
as he meditated. We seriously doubt if true
love were ever eloquent at first. The fear of
the very possibility of failure checks the utterance. Ernest and Constance had walked on
for some time in silence until they stood alone
two diminitive specks on the long line of coast
clearly revealed in the moonlight. At any
other time the transcendent beauty of the objects
which surrounded them would have inspired
Ernest, but to-night he felt it impossible to
speak of any subject but that which sat so

closely at his heart: his love to Constance
Fairweather. The silence at length began to
grow oppressive to both. Miss Fairweather
repeated her former question, but with a less
confident tone than before. " And you cannot guess what I have to say ?" replied Ernest,
thinking it absolutely necessary to say something.

" No indeed, why are we here ?"

" Why are we here Constance ?" he repeated
mechanically, " to—to—admire the beauty of
nature—to unburthen my mind of a secret which
but that I think you must already guess it and
that you are departing in a few days I would
not have dared to breathe so soon, to tell you,
bright angel, that I love you."

Miss Fairweather appeared really agitated
and to find some difficulty in speaking. At
length she said,—

" Let us go."

" Not till I hear from your own lips my fate."
He threw himself at her feet and grasped her
hand. " I have been frank with you Constance,

be equally so with me. Oh what would you, could you, have thought of me, if I had not told you this after the happy hours we have spent together. Have you no word for me. Tell me at least you are not angry, that I have not offended you by this disclosure, one word to rid me of this suspense."

" Oh Mr. Basil, what need of words. Have I not made my feelings quite apparent already."

And Ernest rose the accepted lover of Constance Fairweather and clasped her to his bosom.

*　　*　　*　　*

At length they could both, speak but what words could paint the brightness, the joy, which dwelt within their hearts. Yet happy moments must have an end, and even that delightful, memorable walk could not now be prolonged.

" Who would have thought it, we are at the gate already. Must we separate so soon?" " Not a minute longer. " Well if it must be so :—But I can call to-morrow."

" No pray do not come to-morrow."

" But you will be out walking and I shall see

you here, or we will meet at the library." For one brief instant their lips met and then Miss Fairweather had vanished through the postern.

Slowly and thoughtfully Ernest bent his steps towards home. " There is a tide in the affairs of man." What possible influence might the events of the last hour have upon his future destiny? and it was all true, it was no dream, there was no doubt henceforth. He knew that Constance loved him: from her own lips he had heard it. Was not that dear delicious avowal still ringing in his ear. Was not her kiss yet warm upon his lip. Then away with any cold doubts of constancy—any forebodings of misery or faithlessness. A strange feeling of exultation arose within his bosom to which he had long been a stranger. He would have given much for some dear friend now, to whom he could pour out his surcharged heart. He had had such a friend once, but he was in his grave. Was it strange that he should think of him at this moment, of the truest friend he ever had or could have, to whom he had ever

turned in joy or sorrow. Was it strange that
at this moment overpowering memories of the
past should crowd upon his soul, causing him
when he had reached home, to sit down and
fairly weep. Thus strangely are joy and sorrow
mingled in our natures.

Mrs. Basil was playing on the piano. She
did not notice his emotion, but it seemed to
relieve him, and he felt happier. Then he
began to write a letter to Constance.

"Ernest, you are not going out to-night
again, surely."

"Only to the post office my dear mother."

Mrs. Basil saw that her son appeared in
unusual spirits, although his eyes looked red,
which she attributed to his having read something which had affected him.

The next day any one who had watched
Ernest closely, would have guessed that something had occurred to disturb the monotony
of his existence. He was fidgetty, yet in perfect good humour, seemed to have a great many
letters to write, starting up every now and then

to look out of window, and took a greater interest than usual in the arrival of the postman.

In the course of his wanderings he strayed as usual into Mr. Stewart's room, and found there very much to his surprise Miss Lawrence. He was on the point of going up to her with his usual frankness and enquiring when she had come in, but was deterred by observing that she was quite pre-occupied and did not notice his presence, as she sat leaning her head on her hand in a somewhat melancholy posture. He had even turned to withdraw, surmising that he might be an intruder, when Miss Lawrence raised her head suddenly, and in spite of the involuntary smile which lighted up her features, he perceived she had been weeping.

" Pray excuse me," began Ernest, and then stopped, thinking it would be better to take no notice of her emotion.

" Don't go Mr. Basil, it's nothing," said Miss Lawrence, though not without embarrasment. " I was only *greeting* a little at the thoughts of leaving my kind friends here."

" You surely do not mean that you are going so soon ?"

" My father is coming to fetch me to-morrow; and though I am returning to a happy home, yet I have been so happy in Y——, that you see how sorry I am to leave it."

" And your departure will make others sorry too.   I for one, owe Miss Lawrence a debt of gratitude, for the happiness I have derived from her society.   Here the Misses Saunders entered the room, and great was the quizzing which Ernest had to endure about his last night's walk with Miss Fairweather."

" Where could you have been all the time, Mr. Basil ?   You left here at eight o'clock, and did not return till half past ten.   Did you lose your way, or did you find Mrs. Grainger's society so agreeable ?" said Miss Saunders.

" And what good spirits he has been in all day," said the youngest.

" What will you do when she returns to the country ?   She is going in a few days."

" Perhaps he will follow her."

"O, of course, I must," said Ernest, " if I am so severely smitten."

" And don't follow her, unless you are, said Miss Saunders, gravely.

" Like most men in love ; this sort of teasing was not at all disagreable to Ernest."

" What," said he, " Would you have me run away from captivation ? You forget my motto—Never to be afraid of any woman."

" O, I make no doubt," said Miss Saunders, " You can manage to forget *her* as you have done many others ; but *she*, poor girl, may never see any one in her future existence that she can like as well."

" There, you touch me. I would not be vain enough to originate such an idea. You must give us men credit for a little humility, as well as selfishness. Rather than you should imagine me such a heartless being, I would imprecate on myself the doom of the false knight—

" In the lost battle born down by the flying,
Where mingles war's rattle with groans of the dying,
There *let me* be lying."

" Well," said Miss Saunders, " I don't know, you may have a heart."

" You think time will show, I suppose?" said Ernest, laughing.

Captain Lawrence spent that evening with them. As we shall give a more particular description of him by-and-by, we shall merely say at present that he was a fine old naval officer retired on half-pay, living contentedly on a little farm at Abercorn, about fifty miles from Y——, and not overburthened with wealth. He seemed quite pleased to make the acquaintance of Mrs. Basil and her son, and gave Ernest a cordial invitation to pay him a visit at Trafalgar Cottage, which Ernest accepted without the most remote idea of ever being able to fulfil it.

The morning fixed for Miss Lawrence's departure had arrived ; and so well did Ernest appreciate the kindness and frankness of that young lady, that in love with Miss Fairweather as he was, he felt very sorry she was going. He was talking to Miss Saunders in Mr.

Stewart's room, when Alice, the younger sister,
came running in, followed by Miss Lawrence,
who appeared eager to prevent her from
speaking.

" I will never forgive you Alice, if you do ;
but Alice was not to be restrained."

" Oh, do you know Mr. Basil ? Elinor wants
a lock of your hair, and she's too bashful to
ask for it, so I said I would—that's all."

" Oh, Alice," exclaimed Miss Lawrence,
while tears of vexation stood in her beautiful
eyes. " How could you. Pray Mr. Basil
don't mind her, it's just a foolish joke."

" You know very well you said so to me a
long time ago, when you first came," said
Alice, " and what is it after all to cry about ?"

" I am so ashamed, Mr. Basil—what must
you think ?"

" Pardon me, Miss Lawrence ; but I perfectly
agree with Miss Alice that there is no occasion to be ashamed of so simple a request. I
esteem it as a happiness, an honor, believe
me, to present such a token of remembrance

to a friend. I only wish it was a more worthy gift, or one that required more merit in the doner."

He said this so politely, in a manner so free from affectation and coxcombry, that Miss Lawrence felt it was better to view the matter in the same light which he appeared to do. So Ernest sat down amid a great deal of laughing, and submitted to the amputation of one of his curls.

" Leave me enough for a scalp-lock," he said, " in case I should go back to America and fall among the Aborigines."

" We must not take this one in front," said Alice, " we must leave this for Miss Fairweather. There, this nice little modest one behind will do. Nobody will know the difference."

" Why," said Ernest, as they held out the trophy, " you have indeed been moderate in your demands. The last time I gave a lock of my hair to a young lady, she left a great bald place on my head. I remember it well from the very strong expressions of disgust it excited in my hair dresser, when I paid him the next visit. But even if I resembled Sampson, whose strength lay in his *capillary* substance, I should feel no perceptible diminution of vigor from the loss of that tiny curl."

"There goes Miss Fairweather," cried Alice, and the suddeness of the movement by which Ernest transported himself to the window, was not lost either on Miss Saunders or Miss Lawrence.

"Some one said she had large feet," continued Alice, "but I don't think so."

"Nor I neither," said Ernest. "I don't think they could be less without being too small."

"What a hurry you seem to be in," said Miss Saunders, wickedly.

"You needn't laugh, I have an important engagement, I assure you."

"I don't in the least doubt it; but don't

forget Miss Lawrence goes at four o'clock to-
day."

"Never fear. I shall be at the coach office
to bid Miss Lawrence good bye."

"Take care you don't meet somebody to
make you forget it."

Ernest had very nearly been too late to see
Miss Lawrence off. When he arrived at the
spot where the coaches were upon the point of
starting, he found a small knot of her admirers
there already, for she had not a few as may be
expected.

"Oh, here he is," exclaimed the Misses
Saunders, "I knew he would come. There
she is, look, in that coach."

And there indeed sat the beautiful Miss
Lawrence, endeavouring with some difficulty to
smile through her tears.

"I shall not forget," said Ernest, "the
kind invitation I have received from your father.
You may see me there sooner than you imagine."

This was spoken at a venture, little thinking how soon his words might come true.

Miss Lawrence's eyes brightened through her tears, an involuntary smile played over her features, and departed as suddenly as it came.

" I think you mean Miss Fairweather. You will not come to Abercorn. You care not if you never see me again."

" How can you make such an unfeeling speech after asking for a lock of my hair," said Ernest gaily.

" You know I could not help that after what Alice said," and then she added, " I wish you would not compliment me, Mr. Basil. I hate the language of praise which does not come from the heart."

Ernest had hardly time to feel surprise at the earnest manner in which these words were spoken, for the coach started, and Miss Lawrence removed the handkerchief from her eyes to flutter it at the window, while Ernest stood gallantly waving his till the vehicle had disappeared.

" Is she not a kind, warm-hearted girl," said Miss Saunders, " I am sorry and yet so glad she is gone."

" Glad and sorry, that is an enigma. May I ask why ?"

" Because I think she was growing too fond of somebody in Y——."

" She had so many admirers that it is not wonderful if she should have been a little smitten with some one or other of them."

" And you really have no idea who that somebody was ?"

" I have sometimes thought it was that tall handsome Mr. Edwards."

" Nothing of the sort."

" Not Mr. Danvers ?"

" Certainly not," said Miss Saunders, in a very decided tone, while a blush at the same time overspread her features, which Ernest could not help remarking.

" And why not Mr. Danvers ?" he said in a rallying tone, which gave the conversation a new turn, and perhaps prevented him from then making the discovery of the party who had engrossed Miss Lawrence's affections.

" And now," said he, as they reached home, " I must go and dress for a tiresome dinner party. Ah, if Constance were to be there."

CHAPTER XII.

IMAGINE then, gentle reader, the change which
has come over the spirit of Ernest Basil's
dream. He, but a few short weeks ago so tired
of life, so *blasé* and *ennuy'e*—now full of hope
and joy, energy, love. Ever since he had gone
home that evening and poured forth his whole
soul in a letter to the only woman he had ever
truly loved, he had indeed been a changed
man. How indescribably happy was he now?
In what occupation did the day glide by into
which Constance Fairweather, either mentally
or personally, entered not? He was either
walking with her, or sitting at the window
watching for her appearance, (for love is so
full of devices that he knew the programme of
her daily avocations with wonderful certainty,

and was constantly meeting her by the merest
chance), or else writing to her, or reading the
letters which she sent him, or else listening
while others talked of her, and slily prolong-
ing the conversation upon this interesting topic·

The dear, the delightful, the ever-precious,
never to be sufficiently prized letter he received that morning. In it Miss Fairweather
had signified that she was going to take tea
at a certain house, and that if he should be
out walking about half-past five, they *might
meet by chance.* It is a fact that Ernest was
out walking at that hour, and that they did
meet, and though the near approach of Miss
Fairweather's departure began to be felt by
both, yet they could not be otherwise than
happy in each other's presence. The very
obstacles and difficulties under which they met,
gave a zest which a more ordinary course of
wooing would not have possessed. Surely
there is something peculiarly pleasant, if not
romantic in walking beside a young lady to
whom you appear in the world's eye a mere

ordinary *beau*, knowing that your hearts are knit together by a *bond of sympathy* which causes you to look with pain upon even a temporary separation.

How peculiar too is the conversation of lovers apparently talking in the most trifling manner to the unconcerned observer, who does not know that there is a free-masonry about love which invests everything, however insignificant, connected with the loved object, with a deep absorbing interest.   Lovers should be at least judged by their peers, that is, by people who are or have been in love, and they will never be convicted of talking nonsense *to one another*. There is a great deal of stuff talked by people who are, not in love, which has this disadvantage compared with lover's nonsense—that it is interesting to nobody.   To staid sensible people who either never marry, or else marry as a matter of business, and who know nothing whatever about love, lover's talk would indeed be as uncongenial a babble as a foreign language, which indeed it is to such.   Yet to

others who regard this powerful passion as one
among other instruments of human happiness
appointed by God, there will appear something
holy and beautiful in the mute or spoken language of lovers, even as in the prattling of a
young mother to her babe.   It is the one universal tongue of nature which has outlived the
confusion of Babel, and now binds all nations
in its irresistible tie, more powerful than all
the little obstacles which human passions and
prejudices have reared up in time ; it is the involuntary homage which we offer to the Creator in worshipping the creature, which causes
two beings to look upon and love one another,
and overlook all imperfections, all blemishes,
and appear to one another robed in that glorious beauty with which the Almighty hand
has invested them ; to re-echo the fiat which
Jehovah pronounced on all the creatures that
he had formed—that they were beautiful and
good.

   " Take care, that is Miss Scunnerweel's

house that you have forbidden me to pass with you," said Ernest."

Oh, no matter, the old maid will be at her tea just now."

Although Miss Fairweather had to go back to the house for a shawl, and though they did not walk very fast, they arrived in Ernest's opinion much too soon at the house where Constance was engaged to drink tea. He had so many things to say to her, all of the highest importance. Must he then resign her to the tender mercies of others who knew not half her value. Must he go away, knowing that she was dispensing her smiles to others.

But did he hear aright that Miss Fairweather had made a solemn compact only to remain till eight o'clock, and Aggy the maid was coming to see her home.

"I'll come too," said Ernest, " and stroll about till I see you come out."

Ernest was so impetuous and self-willed. Miss Fairweather knew him to be so obstinate

when he once took a thing into his head, that
she did not waste time in attempting to alter
his determination. Besides, as he very truly
remarked, how could he trust Miss Fairweather
to Aggy's protection at that hour in the
evening.

Oh, happy Ernest, did neither Mrs. Basil
nor Miss Saunders suspect when you entered
with such a jovial countenance, and enlivened
the tea table with so much good-humoured
nonsense, and appeared so particular to know
whether the clock was exactly right, and started
away precisely at a quarter to eight o'clock, that
you had gone to keep tryst with your lady love.

"Come on, Mr. Basil, and let Aggy alone,"
said Miss Fairweather.

" Just that," said Aggy, in reply to something which Ernest said to her while he slipped
a shilling into her hand.

" I was telling Aggy not to lose sight of us."

But the injunction must have been imper-
fectly understood; at all events, there was
Aggy disregarding it already, and lingering

a long distance in the rear. Perhaps Aggy was artful and had been in love, "*jaloused*" that Mr. Basil and Miss Constance might not wish to be overheard. Certain it is, she showed a great deal of discretion, and very little curiosity in keeping always out of ear-shot. When Mr. Basil and Miss Fairweather walked steadily on she acted as a reserve; when they lingered and stopped as people will do when they talk earnestly, and when she unconsciously came up with them, she passed promptly and became a *vidette* or advanced guard, as the case might be. This system of tactics Aggy unflinchingly observed with almost the regularity of military precision, taking up her position either in front or rear, but at all times hovering at a distance from the main body without joining company.

There is something strangely and romantically interesting in thus walking with the woman you love best in the world through the streets on an evening. Everything wears a charmed changed aspect; nothing looks as it did before.

The buildings which you thought ugly and insignificant, have become palaces—every street is a *broadway*. The lamps emit a strange supernatural brilliancy. The gay shops are like a vision in an eastern bazaar, and you are become a sort of Caliph Haroun Abraschid (only far happier than any king or kaizar) walking disguised through the streets of Bagdad. A matter-of-fact person might object to the rain. Mr Stewart certainly would have thought the damp very bad for the rheumatism.

But you a lover cannot call it a bad night. There is a mist, certainly, a sort of heavy dew, a refreshing moisture. It is as well to put up your umbrella and draw the loved form nearer to you, but it will pass away presently and the stars will shine out, and even if they should not, what matter as long as those bright stars, *her eyes*, shine on you. O, happy lovers, enchanted pair, walking not upon earth, but through the streets of a fairy city. Love, the great necromancer, thĕ wizard of the north, south, east, and west, has bewitched you and

thrown a *glamour* in your eyes. You wonder
if you are the only lovers in the crowd, hurrying past on business, as if business could make
them as happy as yourselves. Is not your joy
contagious? Does it not affect the passer-by?
They only hear a chance word which conveys
no meaning. They cannot tell what is passing
in your hearts. In their eyes you are, we blush
to say it, two mortals, nothing more.

"Constance, your approaching departure
weighs very heavily on my spirits. To think
we are so soon to separate. If I thought it
hard that we should meet so seldom in Y——,
what shall I do when you go to Bonnar?"

"Yes, and while I am *moping* there you,
perhaps, will grow forgetful of me."

"This is the way you write in your letters.
Do I ever tax you with inconstancy? The
truth and sincerity of my affection will not permit me to doubt yours, Miss Fairweather."

"I never told you not to call me Constance."

"Constance, then, dear Constance, you know
how often I have sought your permission to

write to your uncle. You know how mortifying it is to me, to both of us, to have recourse to these clandestine meetings, as if we had any reason to be ashamed of loving one another. Constance, I am poor, but that is no impossible barrier surely to my becoming your husband. By birth and breeding I am worthy of you, and I trust a certain period will prove that in other respects it is not presumptuous in me to aspire to your hand. You have confessed that my attachment is reciprocal. Is not our course perfectly clear? Why hesitate? Would not your uncle if he knew all, look favourably on our hopes? You say he loves you; write to him yourself if you will not let me write, and let your guardian here make every enquiry about me. Our agent will furnish him with all particulars relating to my prospects, &c."

"Ah, Ernest, I don't want to know more about you than I do already."

"I believe you, dearest, but you love me; you look with partial eyes. Your uncle will be more difficult to please; he will only regard our attachment like a man of the world.　O, how I wish the uncertainty was cleared up—if I had some assurance, some hope, now that you are going away—how wretched, how unhappy I shall be, dreading that some influence may come between us and estrange us. I know I shall not be able to exist *here* while you are gone. I must follow you; you must arrange some method for my seeing you in the country."

"Ah, that's just what I fear, that you will follow me, that your impetuous disposition, your want of self-control, will prompt you to some rash step, such as coming after me to Bonnar, and make people talk, and then it will be impossible to meet."

"Never fear, I will do nothing rashly. Only promise me to write immediately on your arrival, and try to arrange some plan for a speedy interview. It is so natural that I should come there to sketch, and if I don't mistake, you are only thirty miles distant from Abercorn, where Captain Lawrence lives, and he has asked me there to pay him a visit, so people will think I am in Abercorn."

"Well, well, we will see. I will try and arrange some plan or other. I have promised a visit to Miss Lawrence, too, only don't be impatient and spoil all."

" And don't forget you are coming to spend Tuesday with my mother, and while we are putting some finishing touches on the picture, we can talk it over."

While conversing they had unconsciously reached the sea-shore, the scene of many pleasant walks. The rain had passed away, and though the moon did not shine, it was a glorious night, a night which the lover of nature would especially admire. The clouds were low, and seemed to brood on the surface of the sea, which without being violently agitated, rolled in its dark waves with a long sullen swell. Ernest drew Miss Fairweather's attention to the brilliant phosphoric light which appeared like a low wall of flame as each wave broke upon the shore.

" Look," said Ernest, " how much beauty is continually lost to mortals.   In that good town there are people preparing even now, from habit, to retire to rest, thinking it sinful to sit up beyond a certain hour, and already tired of themselves and everything else. Try and tempt them out by telling them of such a sight.   See how wave succeeds wave, as if each contained a life which perished in that sudden brightening up and sad moan.   Surely, surely, so much beauty must have been intended for beings more capable of appreciating it than man."

" Hush," said Miss Fairweather, " do not talk that way.   Some people would say it was not *canny* at this time of night, and in this place."

It was certainly a night to be remembered. Along the west yet glimmered a faint line of light, that inexpressibly beautiful tint of the evening sky which painters and poets do so love, cut sharply by a steep promontory which in its strong contrast of shadow might be likened to the material and the present, shutting out the spiritual far-off, typifyed by that evening sky—a passing glimpse only to be recorded by the few imaginative lovers of nature amid the millions of slaves to mammon.

Here then, on the same spot where he had first breathed his affections, the lovers repeated their mutual vows of love. There by the gentle lullaby of the waves, stood these two mortals launching themselves forth from the happy present into the unfathomable sea of futurity, by vows which it is out of their power to keep, of which a few revolutions of weeks, days, or it may be hours, may show the fallacy. Oh, invisible spirits of earth, sea, and air, do you never weary of hearing these magnificent promises made by perishable beings who will, by the flight of time become estranged to each other and to themselves? Did no prescience of coming trouble, of the lightness of woman's vows then intrude in Ernest's heart? Did no whispering of the invisible spirits around, which are called voices of nature, did nothing in the sigh of the wind, or the solemn dash of the wave, or the wild illumination which accompanied it, inspire a doubt of the good faith or constancy of the being who stood by his side? None whatever.

It may, or it may not be deemed a singular circumstance that Aggy (who all the time the lovers were conversing together so earnestly was practicing her manœuvres *as vidette,*) found something very interesting to look at in every direction but that in which the young gentleman and lady stood. Whether Aggy was a lover of nature, or whether she was thus hindering herself from being qualified to give any important testimony in case of being subpœned by Mrs. Grainger as queen's evidence, it is impossible to say.

"Aggy," said Mrs. Grainger, when Miss Fairweather had gone to her own room to remove her out-door habiliments, "tell me at once, was Mr. Basil with Miss Fairweather!"

Thus hard pushed Aggy made answer.

"I'se no deny, mem, that Maister Basil may hae forgathered wi' Miss Constance and just convoyed her home like, but indeed he's a douce gentleman and—"

" Send Miss Constance to me," said Mrs. Grainger.

" Constance," said Mrs. Grainger when they were alone, " I have learned through young Flaccid that you have been in correspondence with Mr. Basil for some time." The good lady did not add that she had intercepted one of that gentleman's letters. " You had better tell me all about it."

There is no occasion to retail the conversation which passed. Suffice it to say, that Constance confessed all to Mrs. Grainger, and received from that lady—such a lecture as might have been expected.

The influence of this *tête-à-tête* on Miss Fairweather's conduct will be partially seen in the next chapter.

CHAPTER XIII.

A CHANGE OF SENTIMENTS. MISS FAIRWEATHER
ACTS LIKE A PRUDENT YOUNG LADY.

IF any one had dared to impugn the faith of
Constance Fairweather, on Saturday night,
Ernest would have defended it as he would
have done a mother's or a sister's. He slept
peacefully that night, little thinking what
mental anguish would intervene, ere he should
again enjoy sweet rest. On Sunday morning
he went forth to church, the happiest man in
Y——, with a letter for Constance between the
leaves of his prayer-book. It was on Sunday
evening that the first cloud appeared in the
horizon of hope. He and Constance were returning from church along with Alec Flaccid,
who seemed to be very pertinacious in inflicting his company, and hindering the unreserved
communication for which Ernest was so anxious,
for something in the manner and words of

Constance, had awakened a suspicion that all was not right. Taking advantage of a moment's *tête-a-tête* unheard by Flaccid, who had been prevailed upon to get out of ear-shot, Ernest exclaimed,—

" For heaven's sake, Constance, what is the meaning of those few words ? In what way do my letters offend you ?"

" Because you write so boldly and confidently, and—and—pray don't ask me to say more to-night; I must go in—do let me go— Mrs. Grainger will wonder what is keeping me "———

" But, Constance," said Ernest, scarcely knowing if he were awake, " whose fault is it that we meet in this way ? Have I not begged and implored leave to write to your uncle? Do you think I do not feel the humility of this false position—of these clandestine meetings both on my account and yours, and which nothing but your plighted troth could sanction ?"

" Ah ! that is it—that is what I wished to

say; it is—in short, do you consider that I am—I mean that I cannot engage myself to you."

Ernest Basil staggered as if he had received a blow.

"Not engage yourself? Then what do all our promises and confessions mean?—our moonlight walks—our *tête-à-têtes*? Can you tell me after Wednesday, nay, after lastnight—"

But here Aggy came with a message from Mrs. Grainger that Miss Constance was to come in immediately. Miss Fairweather uttered a hurried farewell and entered the house, while Ernest rushed from the spot in a tumult of frenzy and despair.

Ernest went to bed miserable enough that night. He lay tossing, and turning in his mind every imaginable supposition to account for the extraordinary conduct of Constance, till at length his own generosity of disposition lulled to rest in a great measure his suspicions, and as he thought over all the assurances she had given of her affection, her image, with all

her beauty and accomplishments rose up before him, as did Desdemona's to Othello—

> " If she be false, then heaven mocks itself.
> I'll not believe it."

Monday passed by, some way or other, without his seeing Constance, or receiving a note
from her, and on Tuesday morning when he
came down stairs, his mother put a note into
his hand.   He tore it open and read as follows—

" Miss Fairweather presents her compliments to Mrs. Basil, and regrets that pressing
engagements will prevent her having the pleasure of spending Tuesday with her."

Almost wild with disappointment, he sat
down and wrote a letter begging, praying for
some explanation of her conduct, beseeching
to be permitted to write to her uncle, adjuring
her to keep her promises, &c.

He hurried off to deliver his letter himself, dreading that unless he took this precau-
tion, Miss Fairweather might never see it.
Miss Fairweather had gone out with Miss Flaccid to *make some calls.*   He went in search of

her, feeling that he must see her and have an explanation, or else go mad. At the door of a shop a cab had just stopped. He arrived in time to hand out Miss Fairweather and Miss Flaccid. With difficulty he succeeded in saying with an affected calmness —

" I have a letter for you, Miss Fairweather, and have just been calling at your house. May I ask why you have not kept your engagement with my mother. ?"

Miss Fairweather was not free from embarrassment, though she seemed calm enough compared to Ernest, as she replied " that she regretted very much the hurry of her departure, farewell visits, &c., should have deprived her of the pleasure, &c., &c."

" Do you go then to-morrow ?"

" No, not till Thursday."

There was at least, then, one day's reprieve, that was something. " And when, then, am I to see you again ?" he said, as he put the letter into her hand.

" If you call at two o'clock."

Oh he would be punctual, never fear. He saw her seated in the cab and breaking the seal of his letter as it drove away. He followed it a short way, till it stopped, and Miss Fairweather got out and entered a house, leaving Miss Flaccid in the cab, who stared very hard at Ernest as he passed, for he had not taken the slightest notice of her whatever. At length he began to reflect that such strange conduct must expose him to public animadversion without being of any possible use. He began to walk towards home like a man in a dream. He met Flaccid, and had some thoughts of kicking him, as he suspected that he had in some way interposed. At last he got home and sat down to *wait*. Would two o'clock never come?

* * * *

When two o'clock did arrive, Constance Fairweather and Ernest Basil were sitting *tête-à-tête* on the sofa in Mrs. Grainger's drawing-room.

When a woman undertakes to tell a man on

a Tuesday that the vows breathed on a Friday are all to be cancelled—that they are but so much empty air— that her love is like—

> " A tale
> Told by an idiot, full of sound and fury,
> Signifying nothing."

That the hopes she had instilled, and nourished, and kept alive in his heart, till they had become like the Polar Star to the mariner— are to be dashed suddenly to the earth and extinguished, how should such a communication be made ?

On the stage where they ape life, tears, and sighs, and passionate ejaculations, and other outward and visible signs of real sorrow, would probably accompany it. But truth is stranger than fiction, as Ernest had a good opportunity of learning that day.

The substance of Constance Fairweather's communication, given doubtless with all the delicacy befitting a young lady, so well and religiously brought up, and *au fait* in all the *bienseances* of society, and with all those be coming feminine airs and graces by which a woman manages to disarm the resentment of the man whom she is torturing and fooling, was to this effect—" That she had thought seriously over the whole affair of their attachment, and confessed all to Mrs. Grainger, and had acted by her advice and her own concurrence in discontinuing all visits, letters, sittings, &c., so abruptly." And so by little and little she managed to tell her amazed lover, with an appearance of pretty girlish interesting grief, *without one single tear*, as he long afterwards remembered, that he must look upon all their vows as cancelled—that the letters which breathed her fondness and expressions of devoted constancy, the looks and words of love which had passed between them meant nothing *now*, and that the events of the past week or weeks had better be eradicated from the memories of both.

There are two or three ways for a hero to behave under such circumstances according to novelists. He may either storm and rave, and accuse his mistress of fickleness, and leave her

overwhelmed with all the epithets due to inconstancy, which an excited imagination can
suggest on short notice; or he may fold his
arms and regard her with a gaze of withering
scorn, and treat her to a few words of bitter
irony, or perhaps assume a demeanour of dis-
dainful passionless politeness, and stride from
the room speechless in cold contempt of one so
false and unworthy as to trifle with her power
over another's feelings, and her own womanly
dignity at the same time; or he may throw
himself at her feet in a fit of passionate eloquent entreaty, and endeavour to soften, by all
the witching supplication of a lover, the severity of her obdurate heart.

But Ernest did none of these things. He
gazed upon her, wondering at the perfect control with which she made announcements so
astounding—so strange and startling. Perhaps the pretty playful way in which the torture was inflicted may have somewhat disarmed
it of its keenness, by suggesting doubts of its
reality. Perhaps she might be only playing

with him, if, indeed, he were not dreaming. No wonder if he found it difficult to believe his senses. Could Constance Fairweather really be saying this in very truth to him, Ernest Basil—Constance, who had so lately taught him how to value a woman's love—Constance, who had walked with him but three days ago in all the trusting confidence of plighted affection?

Was Ernest to go into transports of grief when the heroine was so provokingly calm? The ladies should surely in common politeness be permitted to give the cue to the gentlemen in such matters. Stunned with the overwhelming nature of the intelligence, as well as at the coldness with which it was announced, Ernest was for some time at a loss what to say seriously and to the purpose. Possibly the reader may think the most appropriate remark under the circumstances would be comprised in two words—" Good morning ;" but he must recollect that sincere affection is not like an idle

capricious fancy, which takes flight at the first
excuse offered—

> " Love is not love
> Which alters when it alteration finds,
> Or bends with the remover to remove."

The words which fall from our lips on an occasion of this kind are no true index of the
weight of the blow, or its impression upon our
feelings. The mind is too much disordered by
the suddennes of the stroke properly to understand or measure it, and we for a time speak
wildly and unfeelingly. Ernest had caught
unwittingly the coldness of Miss Fairweather,
and spoke at first in the strain of levity or
irony. A spectator would have imagined it
was some silly trifling difference, a mere lover's
quarrel, to be shortly made up, to become
integrationem amoris, and not the severing of
two congenial hearts, of two human destinies.

" You told Mrs. Grainger all?"

" Yes!"

" And she advised you to give up the correspondence and the sittings?"

" Yes. She said I had been very much to blame in giving you encouragement."

" Then you are acting by Mrs. Grainger's advice in giving me up in this sudden manner? Your affection is not proof against the first cold word of interference ?"

" No, I assure you you are wrong in thinking I have been influenced against my own judgement."

" It is strange that your own judgment should have prompted this sudden decision and caused such a change in your sentiments just at this moment, when you have been confiding in Mrs. Grainger. But, Constance, can you answer to your heart for your conduct? Have you not said you loved me ?"

" Well, I—I—did love you !" spoken with a mixture of coquetry and self-reproach.

" But since Saturday, by taking counsel of Mrs. Grainger, who has not in any way influenced you, you have made the discovery that *you do not*. And while you have been debating about the method of turning me off,

I have been in a state of miserable suspense ever since you thought fit to raise the first doubts on Sunday evening. I suppose, if I had not found you to-day, you would have left Y—— without waiting to see me again."

" No—no, indeed I would have written."

" Are you quite sure your adviser would have sanctioned it. I admit it would have been kind and considerate, and merciful, but would it have been *proper* according to Mrs. Grainger's views of etiquette, for a young lady so far to follow the dictates of her own judgment as to put her lover out of suspense? Well, you have followed good worldly counsel. Some foolish people will think you wanting in *constancy*, but that is nothing. Doubtless you have the approval of your own conscience. Let me congratulate you on having overcome the struggle between duty and affection, if there was a struggle. It certainly does credit to your powers of will. When next I fall in love, it shall be either with a decided blonde— fair hair and blue eyes, or a decided brunette.

" Oh, but you do not feel it so very much,
do you? It will not make you wretched ; it
will not be such a disappointment as your
irony would imply."

" Why, Constance," said Ernest, in a hollow
voice, " what reason have I now to believe in
any woman, since—"

" I am so *very, very* sorry, I have behaved
shamefully I know—I do not attempt to ex-
tenuate my conduct. I shall not forgive myself in a hurry ; but, you do not—hate—me.
You will try and not—hate me, and after all,
don't you think—you will soon be able—to
forget me."

And as she spoke those words, she must
have known she was inflicting superfine agony.
Forget her while she   sat there *radiant in
beauty*. The witchery—the strange witchery
of a beautiful woman. He held her hand as
she sat beside him there. And her head re-
clined on her bosom, and she looked up into
his face with a half-imploring, half-coquettish

glance, as if she fully knew her power, and knew him to be her slave; while her long ringlets, partially dishevelled, fell down in luxuriant beautiful disorder over her breast.

"I am afraid I shall find forgetfulness a far more difficult task, than you appear to do, Constance."

"You have a right to reproach me. My own heart will do so for many a day. I cannot account for the sudden change in my sentiments; but—it is better to have pain now, than misery hereafter. At least, I will be frank now. I am not my own mistress. I am not of age. I had no right to answer for the future, or dispose of myself. You took me by surprise when you spoke to me of love that night. In a brief delirium, I spoke words which I must now retract, and which you must—and will—excuse."

They conversed together for a good hour and a half.

Ernest had risen, and moved towards the

door. She clung to him, and seemed unwilling that he should part in anger. At length he spoke—

"I could almost curse those who have tampered with your better feelings, and inspired those grovelling doubts and mercenary considerations, Constance, you will not find a man every day to love you as I do. Sincere hearts are not so plentiful that they should be trampled on and abused. Your esteem Constance—the esteem of a heart and mind like yours made me prouder, and raised me more in my own estimation, than I have ever been before. I felt that in winning your love, I had indeed made a conquest, of which I might be proud. We have known each other for a period of four months if our acquaintance is to be estimated by time alone. But we knew one another better in a week, than many people do after the conventional intercourse of years. We have corresponded and laid our hearts before each other. I found I cherished for you a feeling warmer than friendship, and though I feared the avowal was somewhat premature, yet for certain reasons, I delayed not to come and lay my homage at your feet. I offered you my poor heart. I would have waited, Constance, for you for years. You accepted it apparently with joy. Tell me not, I took you by surprise, though I never spoke out before that evening. You must have seen how I loved you. Women are quicker in these things than we are. It is a week since we have been on the footing of plighted lovers, at least, God knows I had every reason to suppose so. Do I dream? Were all those testimonies to my worth which I have at home, in your letters mere empty compliments? Am I not the same man? If any one has slandered me, let me know who your informant is—that's all. Is my heart—are your feelings to be trifled with in this way? *Can you* transfer your affections so easily? Can you plight them and recall them at every breath of caprice. Constance Fairweather, by all that is holy and good, by that avowal of love which has us passed between, and which in the

eye of Heaven, constitutes the marriage of true
minds, though, as yet, we have not sworn before witnesses to love.   Be faithful and true—
to me your affianced.   For the present, farewell.   I am faint and weary. I can neither talk
nor reason further; but we have all to-morrow.
I will write to you ; and let me implore you, by
the love which you say you did bear to me, and
which I still bear to you, answer it before you
go."   With these words, they parted ; and as
the door closed behind him, a dead weight
seemed to fall upon his heart, and he took his
way through the now joyless streets with a sense
of deep overwhelming desolation, such as
his heart had long been a stranger to.

To go home—to say to his mother—" It is
all over now between Miss 'Fairweather and
myself, to hear the maddening advice always
ready on such occasions. " Forget her she is a
heartless girl."   To sit down, take up a book
mechanically, and then to feel that the source
of pleasure, the usual daily routine of life is
dried up, that things which pleased yesterday,

are now weary, flat, stale, and unprofitable—to experience the heart-wearying conciousness prompting a wish that for the next few months, life might be one eclipse of thought and memory, that you could drink of some Lethe, and forget all which has so seared and riven the heart, and made the very name of love detestable; but that the heart having once exerted its mastery over the judgment, memory will continue to whisper—Aye, but you do love her —and picture with the refinement of a demon, the evening you first saw her, every little incident which marked your acquaintance—all the little misunderstandings which threatened its interruption, and your blind and foolish joy when they blew over. What is it prompts you to go up to the studio and look at her picture ? There she stands before you in all her beauty, every graceful attitude, every kind word, every bewitching look, every loving smile remembered —the songs she sung, you run over till past happiness almost makes you forget present misery ; and then the full tide of blank despair begins again to flood the agonised heart. Oh, misery, this was the hour you were wont to meet her, and feel the heavenly influence of her voice, and glance stealing over your spirit. You need not start from your chair—put down your hat — where would you go? It will never be again. There is no joyful meeting in store for you. Roam the streets till you are tired. Constance can still smile; but her smile is not for thee. Her beauty is not for thy gaze—memory, it is madness—forgetfulness, it is impossible. Better banish thought altogether. Cease to think for a time of anything. Be wild, excited—fly to the wine-cup, commit any folly rather than sit still and let that terrible melancholy steal over you. Some have gone crazed with such a disappointment. Arouse thyself, man ! get through this terrible evening. Put time, the comforter between thee and thy misery.

No, it is not over yet between thee and Miss Fairweather. The halcyon days of hope and joy may be over; but the wretchedness of

blighted hopes and unrequited love is only
beginning.   What man thou hast experienced yet but the bright side of love!   Forget, indeed, thou wilt treasure every look and
loving incident—every spot hallowed by her
presence — every token connected with her,
though each link of memory be sharp as the
point of a dagger.   Does the mourner heed
the comforter, who tells him not to grieve for
one o'er whom the sod has just been laid? The
generous spirit still clings sorrowfully to the
empty shrine.

CHAPTER XIV.

A REVELATION—A LOVER'S REMONSTRANCE AND THE
LADY'S REPLY.

O wine thou art a "good familiar creature,"
but thou cannot always dispel care! Ernest
and Danvers sat opposite one another at a
table covered with bottles and glasses. Both
had evidently drank freely, but the wine had
taken a very unequal effect on both. Ernest
showed no symptoms of conviviality, his face
was pale as death, his eyes blood-shot, and his
manner varied alternately from fits of moody
silence to a wreckless humour, extravagant, and
startling from its vehemence. Danvers was
evidently in that happy state when a man likes to
unbosom himself to his friend. He had already
told Ernest half-a-dozen times in confidence,
that he loved Miss Saunders, that he felt pretty
sure Miss Saunders loved him, that he had
been on the point of proposing several times

but always thought it better to postpone it. Somehow he felt particularly confident to-night. It was a pity to put it off—he felt such a flow of ideas, such courage. Thus he ran on about Miss Saunders's beauty and accomplishments, pointing out a thousand little feminine airs and graces, quite ignorant of the torture he inflicted upon Ernest, whenever the latter was not so absorbed in his own reflections as to listen to him.

" I don't ask you why you are so low, Ernest, for you told me that you felt hipped to-night and that you would be wretched company, but I do wish you would cheer up a bit, I have seen you infinitely more lively on the strength of a single glass of punch, and all that you have taken to-night seems to have no effect whatever. It is a sin to keep such a grave face over such good liquor ; which will you take, wine or brandy."

" Brandy," said Ernest, as he poured a goodly portion of the liquor into his tumbler, qualifying it with very little water.

"Well that is a stiff one, you must have a strong head Basil," continued Danvers. "Did you ever know two people give the same cause for drinking a glass of grog. Some drink for good fellowship, because they are in company; others because they are lonely; some must have a dram to raise their spirits, others must have one because they are in such good spirits already. Some like a drop of something ' short and hot,' because it's cold, others like a drop of something cooling because it's so warm, some think a glass will do them good, and others say it will do them no harm, some take it as a medicine, others as a cordial, some as a strengthener, some to make them fat, others to make them thin; some take it moderately on principle, others immoderately without; some because their fathers did so before them; some because it is not forbidden; others because it is, some take it as a necessary stimulus; others to keep the cold out of the stomach, but nobody, strange to say, *drinks* because he *likes it*."

"Come," said Ernest with a suddenness which made Danvers start, "*I will* shake off this melancholy. To prove I'm in earnest, here's a song for you. And he sung in a voice which had melody in it and with a sort of fierce energy, the following lines of Byron—

" Fill the goblet again, for I never before,
    Felt the glow which now gladdens my heart to its core.
    Let us drink, who would not, since thro' life's varied round,
    In the goblet alone no deception is found·

    I have tried in its turn all that life can supply,
    I have basked in the beam of a dark rolling eye ;
    I have loved—who has not, but what heart's can declare,
    That pleasure existed while passion was there.

    In the days of my youth when the heart in its spring,
    And dreams that affection can never take wing;
    I had friends—who has not—but what tongue will avow,
    That friends, rosy wine, were as faithful as thou.

    The heart of a mistress some boy may estrange,
    Friendship shifts like the sunbeam—thou never cans't change;
    Thou grow'st old, who does not—but on earth what appears,
    Whose virtues like thine still increase with its years.''

" Thank you," said Danvers " and very well sung, but do you know your eye looked so wild that I almost like you better in your quiet mood, than when you seem to make such an effort to be gay. I'll give you a more sentimental one than that." The song which he sung happened to be a favourite one of Miss Fairwea-·ther's, and often had Ernest heard her sing it.

Ernest sat with his face covered with his hands, as the song proceeded the tears forced themselves through his fingers, and in spite of all efforts at restraint, his chest began to heave with convulsive sobs.

" Come," said Danvers, breaking off abruptly, " it is late, let us go." and the two young men sallied out presently arm in arm.

They had not advanced far up Grafton street, when they found the pavement occupied by a small crowd which even at that hour, had gathered round an unfortunate female who seemed to be dying.

" Stand awa frae round the lassie.—Rin for a doctor—tak her to the hospital,"— and sundry other suggestions were thrown out in quick succession, but no one moved, and, but for the opportune interference of Ernest and Danvers, the sufferer would have probably perished on the spot.

She was young and too well dressed to leave any doubts as to the nature of her livelihood, and appeared in the last stage of a consumption. Through the instrumentality of Ernest and Danvers she was removed to a neighbouring public house, and a doctor sent for, who pronounced her case hopeless. She might die that very night, or linger on for a week or two, it was impossible to say. " I can do nothing here," said the doctor, " she may want to see a clergyman, perhaps."

The poor girl made a sign as if she wished to speak, and Ernest bent down over her.

" I ken weel," she said, " I'm no lang for this warld, but I canna gang till I ease my mind of a sair, sair burthen."

" Let me send for a clergyman," said Ernest.

" Aye, aye, you may send, but you winna find them ower ready to come to the likes o' me," she said bitterly. " Ye baith seem kind gentlemen. Ye'll mind bonnie Ellen Douglas wha bided in the little cottage as ye gang up the brae. Tak down my words, for what I hæ to tell will clear her guid name, and show how deeply she was wranged."

Danvers had already gone in search of a clergyman, the doctor had taken his departure, and Ernest, taking out his pocket book, prepared to write down her communication.

"I was once a good honest girl," she said, "and if I hadna listened to a villain, I might hæ been sæ still. There wad be na need of mentioning his name as far as I am concerned, but you couldna understand unless I told you, that the same evil doer wha ruined me, and did his best to make Ellen Douglas appear what she was not, was Mr. Pennywise Close. Maybe ye hæ heard of him. There's na a baser hypocrite, or ane that has more mischief to answer for, living now.

"There was aye a rivalry between me and bonnie Ellen Douglas. Me and another ane, Maggy Nicols and her workit at the same manty-makers thegether. Well, one day Mr. Close askit me to introduce him to Ellen. I did sæ, for I was proud to let her see I had got a gentleman for a wooer, and never thocht that anything would happen, for Ellen was an awfu' proud lassie,

and mair than that, she had a lover then, a
likely young fellow, who was educate for the
ministry. Well, time wore away, and Ellen
sundered wi' her lover, I dinna weel know what
for, and he ganged awa' to foreign parts, and
me and Close fell out, and at last he wadna gie
me ony mair assistance, and I lost my situation
at the manty-makers, and things went frae bad
to worse, till at last I became what ye see. At
last rumors began to gang about him and
Ellen Douglas, that made me hate the lassie
mair than ever, and increased my deadly ran-
cour to that degree, I wad hæ done anything
to be revenged, for I thought it was aw her
fault that me and Close had fallen out thegither. Aweel, in this hour the tempter came
to me in the shape of Mr. Close, and he tellt
me how Ellen and he were privately married
by the Scotch Law, and then when he found
me sæ enraged again' Ellen Douglas, he made
me an offer of a vast of money, gin I would
help him to destroy the proofs of the marriage,
and when he saw me willing aneuch to hearken

through my jealousy, and my poverty, and my love of revenge, he tellt me ane of the witnesses was already dead, and there was only a bit paper in Ellen's possession that could prove they were man and wife. Well, na to mak a long story, I consented to do his wicked bidding, and I bided and bided until at length the opportunity came, and I got the bit paper. May God forgie me, I took the only proof the puir lassie had o' her innocence. Well, as ane sin breeds another, I cast about how I could turn it to my ain better account, and I had the paper copied by a clever chiel, and I made Close promise he wad burn it afore ever I gave it till him, which he was ready aneuch to do, and he threw the copy intill the fire without suspecting the cheat, and I keepit the true paper, little thinking then o' righting puir Ellen, but that I might keep the upper hand wi' Mr. Close. Well, when puir Ellen discovered her loss, she was like to gang demented, and she begged and prayed Close to clear her fame with the warld and confess the truth, na for her sake but for his ain bairn's ; and when he would na, the last words she uttered were a curse on a' who had con-spired to ruin her, and she swore that if her child perished through want or cold, or any illness brought about by his neglec, she wad seek out the dastard father and stab him to the heart.   From that day to this I hæ heard na tidings o' her, but weel, I ken, her curse has fa'en heavily on me, and a' the gowd I got by my wicked action has helpit to sink me deeper and deeper intil perdition,   And only this very evening I followed Mr. Close in the street and fleeched sair for a little siller, and he flung me frae him and wadna listen, and when I gied him a glint about the paper o' Ellen's marriage he ca'ed me ' liar,' and struck me, and I fell on the pavement, and he was but just gone when ye cam up."

Such was the account which Ernest care-fully noted down, when Danvers returned to say that he had called on several clergymen, who had refused their attendance on various

pleas. One of them seemed to be afraid of
bringing back some contagious disease to his
family; another had declined on the strength
of the woman's previous abandoned character ;
another on the ground that she had lately become a Popish convert. Ernest showed Danvers the account which he had written down.

"This must be attended to at once," said
Danvers. "My friend Harrison, the advocate, lives close by, I will have him here directly."

He went, and returned in a very short time
with the advocate, who read aloud to the sick
woman all that Ernest had written, adding "the
deposition of Martha M'Foy." As the girl was
too ill to write her name, she made her mark,
and Ernest and Danvers signed as witnesses.
As the sufferer seemed somewhat relieved by
the disclosure, and inclined to sleep, Ernest,
after thanking the advocate, and putting some
money into the landlady's hand, with directions
to provide a nurse for Martha, and take every

care of her, went home with Danvers, meditating on the strange occurrences of the evening.

In the morning his own troubles almost banished from his recollection the events of the previous evening.   He sat writing the greater part of the day, desisting from time to time, as the fervour of his feelings overcame him, and the tears blinded his eyes and fell upon the paper.   At length he produced the following letter to Constance :—

"My Dear Miss Fairweather,—

"Imagine the convulsed state of my mind when I am at a loss whether to pour out the unrestrained feelings of my affection, or to upbraid you as the destroyer of my peace.   Are you the same Constance who on this day week acknowledged a reciprocal feeling of affection for me—who wrote thus : ' that from the first moment you saw me you wished to win my love'—who trusted that time would teach you to forget your love for me, and gave yourself up to the enjoyment of the present without more thought of the future—and who

confessed that when you went in that night, the
tears you shed were tears of gladness—who
could write as follows : ' are you sure you love
me ?—are you not deceiving yourself and me
too ?   Could you truly value my love so much
as to feel happy in the possession of it ?   If I
could only persuade myself that we do love
each other—that you think of me when I am
gone, with feelings as loving as those with
which I shall think of you.   It is too great
happiness to be real.   I shall ever remember
my feelings when I heard you say 'I love you.'
another hour of happiness like that which I
experienced last night will never be enjoyed by
me.   I fear it was the first time I cared to hear
I was loved.   I cannot think of being perhaps
forgotten by you very soon without a feeling of
agony which I should in vain attempt to describe.   Shall I have reason to rejoice that we
met, and that I gave my heart to you, or will
it prove the trial of my life ?   I am sure I have
written nothing that I wanted to say.   I could
not tell you how great my love for you is.

Time will show you the sincerity and constancy of my attachment.' This was written only on Thursday last. On Friday you say : ' You must tell me whenever you begin to think of loving another. I shall never believe it until you tell me yourself, and you must not keep me in suspense by getting colder and colder by degrees ; but tell me at once when you cease to love me. When I said you were not my ideal in everything, I meant that you did not love me. I had always made that an essential item when I thought of my ideal. I know you will think this letter very cold, but I cannot write as you do. You know, however, that my love for you is great—you know that you are the first whose confession of love really interested me. But I think, *dearest*, you will find that I am so difficient in many things that your love for me will change, and then *what shall I do ? I feel that I am capable of loving constantly ; and that if you change, I shall be miserable. May I stake my happiness on your love.* If you knew how I long to be with you to tell you how I love you—to soothe and cheer you when you feel depressed and sad, and to hear in return that you love me. I can imagine no greater bliss than that. Many thousand thanks for your delightful letters. How I treasure them. I must conclude, and do so with every assurance of affection and sincerity. I hope to hear from you on Sunday. Believe me, ever your loving Constance."

" Do you, a moral, accountable being, a Christian young lady, think yourself at liberty to break such solemn promises as you have made ? Does not your sense of right and wrong tell you that they are binding at least until absolved by your uncle and guardian ? I asked for no more than your love. I knew I had no right yet to ask you to unite your fate with mine, whatever hopes or expectations your promises of affection may have given me. None but your uncle could decide on this point; but your affections *were* under your own control: and when you said you loved me, *I believed you.* Time, you declared would prove your sincerity. *Time alone* should have shown the insincerity of your vows, or changed your sentiments on a matter of such delicacy and such importance to the peace and happiness of two hearts. Had those promises been sincere, how could the advice of a third party cause you to cancel them immediately? Is it only a vow made before witnesses that is binding? Are the solemn voluntary promises of two immortal beings nothing, (because they have not been exchanged at the altar) but so much breath to be violated on the first opinion offered by another without even a decent show of hesitation and delay. I shall leave Y—— to-morrow for a few days. A change of scenc is absolutely necessary, both for my physical and mental health. Will you, therefore, Constance, send your reply to this, to-night? Surely you will not be hindered from doing this. And oh dearest for such I can still conscientiously call you, will you be kind and considerate in your reply. Put yourself in my place. Think what my sufferings are and will be. Why should I blush to confess that I can hardly see this scrawl for my tears. Oh, how different from the tears of joy shed this day week, after declaring my love to you. Forgive me for saying you have done wrong in playing with a heart and affections like mine. I will always think of you at the best, and believe it was not premeditated, and that you were influenced by others. Give me some hope. You are very young yet—you hardly know your own mind. Let me know your address in the country, and give me your uncle's abroad, so that I may have it in my power to write to him if I wish. It is the last chance remaining, and in the present state of things, cannot possibly do harm. Recollect that I have never recalled my promise, that I proffer my love as sincerely, as devotedly as ever. Once again I repeat at the close of this letter, those words which one brief week ago, you said caused you such perfect happiness. *Dearest* believe me with the same truth as then, I love you."—E. B.

Ernest carried this letter himself. He saw

Miss Fairweather and held a brief dialogue, as follows :—

"You will answer this to-night?"

"Yes."

"You go to-morrow at seven o'clock?"

"Yes."

"I shall see you at the Coach Office then, for I leave Y—— at the same time."

"Are you serious? You had better not go to-morrow—pray don't."

"I shall go mad if I remain here."

"In what direction do you go?"

"Perhaps to Abercorn, to visit Captain Lawrence. I have not yet decided."

"I hope you will not come to Bonnar."

"I will make no promises."

"*If you do, mind I will not speak to you.*"

"Shall I get your answer to this letter to-night?"

"Yes."

"I will see you then in the morning; till then, good bye."

Miss Fairweather's reply came that evening.

He opened and read, and his face grew of an ashy paleness, his limbs tottered, and he sank on the sofa.

Miss Fairweather had said all that a properly brought up young lady could say under the peculiar and somewhat equivocal circumstances in which she had placed herself, without at the same time altering one tittle of her resolution. As a specimen of this kind of letter may be useful to young ladies wishing to extricate themselves from similar difficulties, we give a summary of it.

Miss Fairweather wrote how unimaginably painful the perusal of his last letter had been to her. It had shown her her conduct in its true light—how wrongly—how wickedly she had acted—not in breaking those solemn promises, but in having ever made them. When her uncle left her, he had exacted a solemn promise not to give her love to any one until his return. How had she kept this promise? Ernest thought her influenced by others. In this he was mistaken. *He* had taken her by surprise when he declared his love. *In the impulse of the moment*, she had written and said things which, on calm consideration, seemed quite wrong.

The letter continued thus :—She had not considered the importance of the words she had uttered—she had *forgot* that they would be cherished, treasured, and remembered, that she was answering for the future instead of keeping to the present—" which alone is ours." She repented bitterly that she *did* confess her love for him—she repented bitterly that she had made those solemn promises which she must now retract—yes *must* retract. Did he think it had been no sacrifice to her to give him up ? Did he think she did not participate in her feelings of misery ? Did he not know and feel that if she consulted her own feelings that she would yet fulfil these vows ? Did she not feel keenly the sin of which she had been guilty ? She was convinced he did not think it would have been different had he been a *wealthy suitor*. She had no desire for wealth,

nor should she ever become the vile thing that
could marry for money. She was happy, and
proud to think that he too was above those
considerations. She knew him to be quite in-
capable of speculating on the worldly means
of the woman he loved. But she felt in all
sincerity, she was not fitted to make him happy.
She thought he knew her better than to think
worldly considerations would interfere with her
love. She felt that she could not exculpate
herself; that he must think her heartless and
deceiteful; for she could not account for the
sudden change which had come over her feelings. She did love him still; but she felt that
for her happiness and his, she must give up
that love. She could not think of it without
great pain; a thousand times that day she had
felt inclined to call on him. She could not
give her uncle's address. She knew he would
not further his (Ernest's) wishes, and she did
not wish him to be in any suspense. Painful
as it was to her to give up all the golden
dreams, she had indulged of becoming the wife

of a Poet, and an artist—of one whom she had such reason to love and admire, still she must say she would rather do that, than hold out to him hopes which could never be realised. Did he think he could be happy with one who wanted exactly the same qualities as he did—self-control, perseverance, and energy. She had no right to speak to him her mind; but she did think he wanted those qualities, and so did she. But she could not dilate on this painful subject. She begged him to think anything of her rather than that she wished to trifle with his feelings. All her faults had originated in having so low an opinion of herself, as to think it impossible that he could love her. She begged him not to hate her—not to think her heartless. She might be foolish and mis-guided. She might be in error even—but she had conscientiously striven to do her duty to him and to herself. Did he think it no sacrifice on her part to give up having a share in the affections of a man whose genius and talent, not to speak of the humane

and charitable disposition he possessed, she admired so much, and whose love she would accept if she dared as the richest jewel the earth
could bestow? Would he forgive her? Would
he say that he would not cherish feelings of
resentment against her—that he would nerve
himself to meet her as a friend—that he would
try and overcome the disappointment for her
sake? Would he not think harshly of her?
It was hard that all was past between them.
She dared not write more. She must say good
bye to him for a very long time. They must
not meet till they could meet as friends. The
servant would call in case he had anything
more to say, because she must not write again.
Did he wish her to return everything? If so,
the girl would leave the parcel and bring back
anything from him. He would not think it
mockery if she bade him seek to be happy.
Good bye again ; would he allow her to sign
herself once (the word more scratched out),
his very loving friend, Constance Fairweather.

Across the letter was written—I will write once
more if you wish it.

Thus ended this precious piece of verbiage.
And for this woman, whose inconstancy and
capriciousness was fully displayed in the glar-
ing inconsistencies of her letter, a man of intellect and generosity felt a deep seated passion.
Far was Ernest from being able to bring to
bear his usual keeness of comprehension on
this letter. He did not even read it all through.
He only saw enough in it to prove death to
his hopes; that he and Constance Fairweather
were devided—that the prop on which he had
leant was stricken from under him—that the
shrine " where he had garnered up his heart"
existed to him no longer. He had been suffering for some time past under severe physical
illness; and this mental blow brought on an
attack of his malady. He lay down on the
sofa, impressed with the idea that his sorrows
were about to terminate speedily with his life.
While he lay in this state, Aggy, the servant

from Miss Fairweather's, was admitted. She brought a package which was to be left in case Mr. Basil had anything to return to Miss Fairweather, and could not suppress a sigh as she looked wondering and half terrified at the prostrate figure so different from the gay lover she had last seen, no later than Saturday, accompanyng her young mistress.

"Tell Miss Fairweather there is no message —no parcel," was all Ernest could utter; and Aggy quitted the room, taking her parcel with her.

CHAPTER XV.

WHILE these events were transpiring in Y——, a young artist (already introduced to the reader) lay stretched upon his bed in an humble street in the city of London apparently in a very reduced if not dying condition; Paul Pearson had come to London intending to proceed to Italy but, owing to pecuniary embarrassments he had been obliged to remain in the city and eke out such a living as he best could by painting landscape, figures, conversation-pieces, and portraits when he could get them to do. Clever though he was, in a strange city without friends, he began to find it at length difficult to scrape together money enough to provide him with the necessaries of life. Sinking deeper into distress, his increasing poverty began at last to tell upon his health.

He was no longer the same gay, handsome student as when first introduced to the reader, a companion of Ernest's in New York. His features grew parched and thin, and the lustre of his eye unnaturally bright, his hand shook sometimes so much that he could hardly hold the palette, or steady the brush sufficiently to paint, yet still he laboured on, supported, as his physical health decayed, by the fire of genius within. It is strange what a triumph mind sometimes exerts over matter. Amid all that penury and distress, the spirit struggled and retained the mastery. He would not yield: he would not die——ere he had looked on the sky of Italy and seen the glories of Michael Angelo.

Reader when you stand in some gallery of art and feel disposed to be unnecessarily severe on the work of some unknown artist, let the biting sarcasm just trembling on the lip remain unspoken. Think that the work before you, may have been the last expiring effort of some child of genius, struggling with penury, illness, and despair, and that the heart which conceived

it has ceased to beat and the hand which exe-
cuted it may be mouldering in the grave. Day
after day the artist sat and painted on some
sweet smiling landscape in the midst of that
crowded city while the pulsations of his heart
grew weaker and weaker and the day seemed
not far distant when the light flickring down
in the socket would be altogether extinguished.

At last he grew so ill that he was utterly unable to paint and was obliged to keep his bed.
His little stock of money was quite exhausted
and he was obliged to pawn picture after picture to procure food and medicines. Mary,
the housemaid, a kind-hearted girl took the pictures to the dealer's or the pawn-shop, and
brought back the money. One day she had
gone on her errand as usual. Pearson had
seemed rather flighty and light-headed in the
morning and she hastened back. Before enter-
ing the room, she heard the sound of voices.
The patient was delirious and talking inco-
herently but he was not alone. By his bed side
was what seemed to Mary, as she afterwards

described it, a white-robed angel of mercy —a beautiful young woman who seemed from the methods she took to soothe the patient to be quite *au fait* in a sick room. She wrote on a slip of paper and handed it along with a piece of money to Mary, who went to the nearest druggist's and returned with a composing draught. It was administered and soon after Pearson fell into a refreshing slumber. The fair unknown, after watching some moments by his bed side put her finger to her lips and walked on tip-toe out of the room, beckoning Mary to follow.

" I am a professional nurse," she said, " and heard accidentally that there was a young artist here who was dying. I do not think there is danger if he has proper nursing and nourishing diet I shall continue to visit him; you seem kind, will you do all that you can for him in the mean time ?"

" That will I ma'am," said poor Mary, with the tears in her eyes, " and oh, if you knew the sorrow I have felt, ma'am, to see him a-growing weaker and weaker every day," here Mary put her apron up to dry her tears. "But indeed, ma'am, that's just what's the matter with him. If he could only afford little comforts, I believe he'd soon be about again. And indeed, ma'am, I once made bold to offer him a small loan myself when he was harder pushed than usual, just to save one of them beautiful picturs. But he's proud, ma'm, for all he's so poor."

"Is he?" said the lady, (for such she might be called without impropriety in spite of her humble occupation) who seemed very much interested in Mary's account of the young artist. "You seem to have a kind heart. And has he no other means of living but by his pictures?"

"None, ma'am. I goes out with them to a picture-dealer's. Sometimes he won't offer anything like their value, and then I takes them to the pawnbrokers. But Lord, ma'am, to think of them elegant picturs goin' for a mere nothink."

" And has he no friends—no resources of any kind ?"

" No, ma'am ; he's a foreigner—an American, and when he first came here, all his talk was about Italy, and he seemed to think it a great hardship to be compelled to stay in London."

" Poor fellow," said the lady, turning away her head. " Take this, Mary," putting some money into her hand, " and buy him a bottle of good port wine, and some arrowroot, and any other little thing that he takes a fancy for—and—don't tell him, Mary, anything about this, you understand ; let him think it is from the pictures."

" And indeed," said Mary, " if I didn't think at the first glimpse it was an angel come down from heaven, as you sat there, with the light shining on your golden curls, ma'am, and indeed it's turned out something very like it, for he'll get well now, I'm sure he will."

Mary was running on with similar incoherent language, when the unknown, giving her a nod and significant look, hurried away.

Pearson awoke much refreshed from his slumber, and as Mary was bringing him a cup of tea to his bed side, he said—

" Mary, I have surely been dreaming, I thought that a beautiful angel with golden hair came and sat beside me at my bed side, and told me I should soon get well. And I remember thinking that death could not be terrible if I could be with her for ever; and then when I put out my hands to touch her, she vanished. I will paint her when I am well enough."

He was still so weak that Mary thought it best to humour the delusion for a while, so she said—

" Perhaps she will appear to you again, sir, if you go to sleep."

" Perhaps she may," said the artist, as he closed his eyes as if to court slumber.

And the ministering angel did come again and again, until the artist was pronounced de-

cidedly convalescent. And between her watchful care and the attention of poor Mary, who
gave up every available portion of her time,
Pearson, though he was at the very gates of
death, was saved, and began to look forward
again to using his pencil, and to indulge in
bright dreams of future fame. Those were
happy days of convalescence, when he was able
to enter into conversation with his beautiful
nurse, who appeared to be interested in his
descriptions of transatlantic life, and looked at
his sketches and pictures delineating forest and
prairie, and scenes so different from those to
which she was accustomed, and listened good-
naturedly to his untiring eloquence connected
with his art. And in these conversations they
grew very well acquainted, before Pearson ever
ventured to ask the name of his preserver. He
was one of those modest retiring characters,
with one bent, who seem intended for nothing
else than artists. He was modest to the very
verge of bashfulness, and had seen very little
of society, and though handsome, was quite

unconscious of his own powers of interesting
or pleasing. He had longed to pour out his
whole heart to his preserver—to tell her that
he regarded her with mingled feelings of devotion and thankfulness due almost to a superior
being; but he had tact enough to discover,
through all his nurse's kindness, a something
amounting to reserve, implying that all advances beyond those of the strict limits of
friendliness would be disagreeable, and he had
abstained from the slightest expressions which
might possibly wound her feelings, even at the
risk of appearing (as it seemed to him) un-
grateful and insensible.

" You are nearly quite well," said his nurse
one day.

The artist's countenance fell; he dreaded
his return to health, which would be the signal
for her departure. The thought of one who
had watched over him with the watchful care of
a mother or a sister in this strange land—of
her going away—of his never seeing her again
—gave him a strange pang which counter-

balanced the joyful anticipations of being once more able to wield the brush.

"I am sure you are glad that you will so soon be able to prosecute your delightful art," continued his nurse. "You have longed so ardently for the time to come. It is a proof that you are wrapped up in your art. It would vouch for your genius even if those pictures did not. You must make haste and become known, and realise your dearest wish of going to Italy."

The painter's heart was melted and his tongue unloosed by the kind way in which these words were spoken.

"Lady," he said, "let me at least know the name of my benefactress."

"You must not eall me lady." said his nurse playfully, "I am but a poor professional nurse—one of the sisters of mercy, and my name is Marchmont—Ellen Marchmont."

"Miss Marchmont," said the artist, "what must you have thought of me that I have never yet thanked you for saving my life?"

" Nay, you must not speak so seriously. I have some experience in sick rooms, and can detect a patient's thoughts by his looks. You have thanked me often and often, though not in words."

" You are kind to say so. I am but a poor painter, who have spent most of my life in rustic out-of-the-way places, and know not how to speak to the purpose. But no speech *could* express my sense of obligation to you, who have saved my life here in a strange country far away from home and friends. Believe me, if I could speak better I should feel less. If there was anything the poor artist could do to show his gratitude—may I not offer you one of these pictures, unworthy as they are, as some memorial of a thankful heart ?—or, perhaps," he hesitated for a moment, and then went on— " perhaps you would like a portrait of yourself better ? I can paint a lady's portrait well, it is next to figure-painting—my forte ; and with such a subject !" and his eyes glistened. He was quite unconscious of flattering Miss

Marchmont—he had no intention of doing so —he only spoke as he felt—the *artist* was aroused. Mentally he was engaged in transferring that beautiful subject to canvass—those light blue eyes—those golden locks—that symmetrical figure. "Ah, what a portrait it will make," he exclaimed, thinking aloud, and then blushing at his own earnestness, and afraid that he had offended Miss Marchmont.

"I shouldn't think of letting you engage in anything so unremunerating at present."

"But," pleaded the artist, "I have no orders on hand."

"Do not be too sure of that, I think I can get you a sitter or too, when you are able to begin, but you must not be in too great a hurry, and I have a lady friend who is desirous to purchase some of your American views. I told her about that beautiful little picture of the Niagara Falls, and she is quite eager to get it. Come now, what do you ask for it."

"Would she think two pounds too much," said the artist timidly.

"Two pounds only for that beautiful picture," said Miss Marchmont, "why, already without seeing it, from my description only, she commissioned me to offer five pounds for it. She said it must be worth that, if it was worth anything. You must not be too humble in your prices. Here are the five pounds;" and she put the money into Pearson's hand. "I will take it with me, it is easily carried, and, though strictly speaking, this should be my last visit as your nurse, yet you must allow me to visit you occasionally in the capacity of a friend, and see what new work you have in hand. Good bye for the present," and without permitting the artist to get in a word, she hurried from the room, leaving poor Pearson perfectly bewildered with amazement, hope, and gratitude.

He recovered rapidly from that time. He began to paint with greater vigor than ever. Sitters began to drop in too, who proved a great trial to his patience, but at the same time enabled him to make a livelihood; but he felt that a change had come over him. He took greater pleasure now in painting a certain face with flaxen ringlets into his fancy pictures, than in the forest and prairie scenes in which he had formerly delighted. His thoughts wandered back less frequently to home and friends; he did not even anticipate so keenly a visit to Italy as he had been wont. He began to think London neither so strange nor so hateful as at first. He began to look forward very anxiously for one of those promised visits from a certain person, and to take consultations with Mary as to the probability of discovering her residence. Whether she ever did come back the reader will learn all in good time, at present we must leave Paul Pearson, to hurry back to Ernest Basil, whom we left in a very critical posture of affairs.

END OF VOL. I.

T. C. Newby. Publisher, 30, Welbeck Street, Cavendish Square.